Bridge

MW00763338

Bridge Ten

By: Harry B. Dodge III

Cawing
Crow
Press

For permission requests, email the publisher, at:
inquiry@cawingcrowpress.com

Published by:
Cawing Crow Press LLC
Dunlo, PA

ISBN: 978-1-68264-024-1

Library of Congress Control Number: 2017930361

Visit us on the web at: www.cawingcrowpress.com

Dedicated to my grandfather, Harry Thomas Folger, with special thanks to my wife Brigid

I

The crowing of roosters from the village grew more urgent as dawn approached. Hal peered down the road, to where he could distinguish individual buildings beginning to emerge from the obscurity of night. He mapped his surroundings as the gathering light revealed landmarks. Exhaling, he could feel muscles held taught during the tense stillness of his watch begin to relax. He wanted to light up a joint. But not yet; he'd wait for full daylight. Instead, he put a tape into the cassette player. *Let it Be* played softly. The song further mediated his dread.

He had spent most of his watch poised tensely, listening. It was the phase of the new moon, and the surrounding countryside was shrouded by an impenetrable darkness. All around him the air was infested with secret noises. Splashing sounds, like something sneaking up the creek, had seized his attention. He'd sat rigid, straining to interpret each subtle water-noise. He thought he sensed a human presence, sly and driven by purpose, but he could see nothing in the night's inky darkness. He had controlled the impulse to fire a flare. That would have brought a call from the Hill. They'd want to know what was going on, why they'd spent a flare, this just after they'd been ordered to lay off the flares because they'd been using them too freely, as if shooting flares was a great form of entertainment. Also, a flare would have awakened Bo, Tennessee, and Sonny. In the case of a false alarm, it would have brought grumbles and cat-calls. So,

Hal had held his own nervous council, and the crisis passed uneventfully. Now, finally, daylight was rapidly gaining the advantage. With the ascendency of light, his night-fears scuttled into the shadows like vampires fleeing the sun.

A thin mist hung over the expanse of rice paddies that stretched westward to the mountains. From where Hal sat, Highway 1 ran south all the way to Saigon, some 350 miles distant. A much shorter drive to the north would bring one to the DMZ. Bridge Ten, the strategic piece of ground they were sworn to defend, could more realistically be described as a large culvert undermining the road. A mile to the south was Bridge Eleven, and beyond that was the Hill, where the highway passed through a narrow defile called Bong Son Pass.

The Hill offered a view of the pass and of the valley floor that stretched north to the horizon and west to the brooding highlands. A dirt road wound to the top of the Hill, where the vegetation had been denuded. There, encircled by rows of concertina wire and claymore mines, were encamped a mortar platoon and the bulk of the Recon platoon. That they, a Recon platoon, were relegated to guarding bridges rather than going out on reconnaissance missions was a sore spot with them all. There were no more reconnaissance missions because the area had been declared "pacified," this the goal of the newly coined Vietnamization process. In reality, however, the area teemed with Viet Cong and NVA. To Hal, the war seemed like a game, where the Americans held control of the countryside by day, but then retired to their defensive positions to allow the Viet Cong to rule the night. The strategy seemed pointless, and the installations had become both sanctuary and prison.

There was a stirring among the sandbags on top of the bunker, and Tennessee's head rose into view. "Oh man," he said. "I had this nightmare.

I dreamed that I was in Nam!"

Hal chuckled, not so much at the stale joke as at Tennessee's appearance: His face was smeared with dirt, and his o.d. uniform, saturated with dust from the highway, was tinted a dull red. The highway's daily traffic lifted a red dust-cloud that impregnated everything within a wide swath. Although the highway was paved, it appeared to be a dirt road, for it, too, was covered with the fine red dust that swirled and fell in a daily cycle. Thus, the men on bridge duty endured dust or mud, depending upon the season.

Hal fingered the wispy mustache he was attempting to cultivate as he watched Tennessee emerge from the shabby obscurity of the bunker. "Might as well open her up for business," Hal said.

They pulled back the strands of concertina wire that blocked the road on each side of the bridge and drug them to the sides of the highway. They returned to the bunker and sat down on the sandbags. Tennessee produced a joint, known locally as a "Bong Son Bomber" due to its healthy proportions, and lit it. They shared the joint and watched the advancing morning.

"Man, I don't like these dark nights," Hal said. He ran his hand through his blonde hair, his fingers serving as comb.

"I hear ya," Tennessee said with his southern twang. His real name was Virgil, but he had acquired the nickname of his home state. He rolled up his sleeves, revealing the tattoo of which he was immensely proud. It showed a pair of jump-boots sprouting wings and suspended from a parachute. *Airborne* was imprinted below the boots. "Another week and we'll have a moon again."

"Yeah, and *three* more weeks, and it's R and R time."

"Right on! Twenty more days and Bangkok here we come," Tennessee responded, and they slapped hands. "I can't wait to try some of that Thai weed!"

"Oh man, I'm not gonna have to hear all about Bangkok again, am I?" Sonny exclaimed, as he emerged from the bunker's interior.

"What are you doing up so early?" Hal asked.

I can't sleep with that Georgia hillbilly sawing wood down there." Sonny was from the ghettos of Washington, DC. With his blue-tinted sunglasses, the once colorful but now faded head-band slanting across his brow, and the thin mustache descending almost to his jaw, far below the military standard, Sonny reminded Hal of Jimi Hendrix.

Sonny took a long draw from the proffered joint. "Oh man," he declared from behind a cloud of smoke, "another beautiful day in the Nam!" He filled his canteen cup from the jug of potable water, lit a heat tab, and began heating water for coffee.

Hal and Tennessee secured their canteen cups and rummaged through the C-ration boxes. Each hunkered over his kitchen fire, adding a packet of instant coffee when the water was hot. Finally, they sat on the bunker and sipped the warm brew.

Sonny opened a can of Ham & Eggs and put it on to heat.

"How can you eat that shit?" Tennessee asked Sonny, who was the only one who would eat the Ham & Eggs dinner from the C-ration selection.

"Mmmm-mmm!" Sonny answered, laughing at their wincing expressions.

Hal and Tennessee settled instead for the canned cinnamon rolls.

The herd of cattle from the village was the highway's first traffic of the day. Three small boys, each clad in shorts and freshly pressed shirt, urged the animals forward. The boys carried sticks with which they occasionally tapped or prodded their charges. The cattle, about twenty head of an identical tan color and bearing the shoulder hump of the Brahma breed, marched obediently, for they were well accustomed to the daily migration. It was necessary to drive them back to the protection of the village each night and then to pasture each

4

morning. The cattle were valuable possessions, and an air of great responsibility was evident on the faces of the boys assigned to watch over them.

The sun was creeping over the low hills that blocked their view of the coast to the east. The light played on the three GIs, and its warmth felt good. They enjoyed the sensation, although they knew this same sun would soon become an oppressive tool of torture.

"Here's Bo," Sonny remarked. "Tired of cutting wood, I guess."

Bo emerged from the bunker and stretched. The first thing one noticed about Bo was the lack of a neck. A large head rested solidly on his broad shoulders without the hint of connective tissue. It gave Bo a sense of slow, plodding power that wasn't wholly inaccurate. Although his name was Gary, he was called Bo because that was what he called everybody else.

"Hey Bo," they greeted him.

"Hey Bo," he replied.

"You're up early," Hal said.

"I can't sleep no more."

"You been working too hard to sleep," Sonny told him.

A lambretta, piled with goods for the market in Bong Son, was the first vehicle to cross the bridge. Lambrettas were the most common civilian vehicles, other than motorcycles or bicycles, and they reminded Hal of enlarged golf carts. Wallowing like a heavily-laden burro, it wobbled across the bridge. Heads from the vehicle's crowded interior craned to look at the soldiers as they passed the bunker. The machine posed a mild disturbance to the road's surface, and dust rose as a languid shadow in its wake.

A milepost stood beside the bridge, bearing signs pointing to: Saigon-350 miles; Washington, DC-10,210 miles; Memphis-9,828 miles; Auburn, NY-10,210 miles; Atlanta-10,620 miles. Similar totems could be found on many of the bridges along the highway.

Two boys approached the bridge from the village. About twelve years of age, they wore sandals, shorts, and shirts of a military-green color. The taller of the two wore a US Army-issue baseball cap. "Hey, man," they said in greeting.

"It's Tim and Tuan, my main men," Sonny replied. "You bring my camsaht?"

Tuan, the one with the cap, smiled and produced a clear plastic bag filled with pre-rolled Bong Son Bombers.

Sonny paid Tuan and received the bag. He took out one of the joints and lit it.

"You beaucoup dinky-dow," the shorter Tim said, laughing and pointing to his head, making a circular motion with his hand.

"*You* beaucoup dinky-dow," Sonny countered. "And me cocky-dow you." He half-rose in feigned ferocity as confirmation to his threat of decapitation.

The two boys shrieked in mock terror and retreated a few steps. "You number ten!" Tim taunted, and they advanced with bravado.

"No, me number one. You number ten," Sonny replied.

"No, you number ten. Me number one!" Tim insisted.

The debate was interrupted when Tuan pointed up the road, saying, "Lifah come. Lifah come!"

They looked up the road toward the Hill, where an angry furrow of dust propheted an approaching vehicle.

"Ah shit!" Sonny growled. He snubbed his joint out, put it back in the bag, and placed the bag under a sandbag.

"You kids dee-dee," Hal shooed them. "Dee-dee mao!"

The boys pranced back to the village, crying, "Lifah come! Lifah come!"

A moment later the jeep roared across the bridge and screeched to a halt in a cloud of dust. "God dammit! How may times I gotta tell you guys to keep them kids away from this bridge?" Sergeant Martin's fat lips worked around the cigar that jutted from his clamped jaw. He arose from the rear seat of the jeep and laboriously dismounted.

"*Keep your fat ass in the jeep*," Bo whispered, and the others suppressed sniggers.

"This is a military installation," the sergeant told them as he advanced. "No civilians are permitted around this bunker or near the bridge. Is that clear?"

The four slouched insolently in silent response.

"I don't want to see this again!"

"What, you gonna ship us to Nam, sarge?" Tennessee asked, and they smiled innocently. Mims, the driver, unnoticed by the lieutenant sitting next to him, made obscene stroking motions. Hal coughed, trying to hold back his laughter.

Sergeant Martin wheeled around, but Mims was scratching his chin and seemed distracted by the view of the distant mountains.

"We have reports of increased enemy activity," the lieutenant announced, "so you men be on the alert. We're on our way to battalion headquarters for a situation report now."

Hal rolled his eyes and winked at Bo. The lieutenant was fresh out of OCS and new in country. With his thin, bookish figure and the "idiot straps" that attached his glasses to his head, he was the object of many jokes.

"We thought this area was Vietnamized, Sir," Cal said, looking confused.

"Well we know better, don't we Jones?" sergeant Martin said. "So you'd better heed the intelligence." He walked back to the jeep. "You're slobs!" he summarized. "I know it's a tall order, but try to look like soldiers."

"Airborne, sergeant!" Bo shouted with military enthusiasm.

The sergeant's back stiffened momentarily, but he continued to swing his body into the jeep. "Okay Mims, let's get outta here."

"What a jerk," Hal said after the jeep had departed.

"You men be on the alert," Sonny said in a falsetto as he re-lit his bomber.

"Yes ma'am," Bo replied, and they laughed raucously.

The day's traffic gradually increased: lambrettas carrying people and goods north to Bong Son and south to Quin Nhon; trucks of ancient French vintage, Viet Nam's closest approximation to eighteen-wheelers, and the disreputable looking truckers, sporting a few wisps of whiskers, wearing shabby straw hats that smelled of tobacco and diesel oil, and the sodden remnants of hand-rolled cigarettes clinging to lower lips; motorcycles driven by the "cowboys," the Vietnamese version of "Easy Rider," wearing an array of black market military attire, and always the sunglasses, ruling the road with cavalier aggressiveness; bicycles bearing one, two, or three riders, sometimes whole families; women hauling loads of various description with wooden yokes balanced on their shoulders and their free arms swinging in unison to the movement of the legs in a fluid galloping lope; and perhaps a rare automobile belonging to a wealthy businessman or a prominent government official. Dominating this domestic traffic, however, were the military vehicles that conveyed personnel and weapons back and forth in a war with no fronts or bounds. Marshaled into vast convoys, the huge grinding machines of destruction raised the road's dust-cloud, making even breathing difficult.

They took shifts guarding the bridge. Sonny had the first watch, Bo went back down into the bunker to resume his nap, and Hal and Tennessee walked into the village.

The village was quiet, almost deserted. This was the time of the rice harvest, and most of the villagers were working in their fields. Those children too young to work were at the school in the neighboring village. Most of the men and older boys were gone, either off fighting or casualties of the war.

Hal and Tennessee's destination was Lay's coke-stand, located beside the road under a clump of large palm trees. Pieces of canvas were stretched over a frame of poles to provide shade from the sun and lend a semblance of structure to the establishment. The coke-stand boasted a large table and a collection of benches and chairs, where travelers sat to enjoy a cool drink and a moment of respite from the heat of their journey. Lay was the proprietress of this, her family's business. She smiled at Hal. "You want a drink, How?" she asked.

"Two cokes, Lay," Hal replied, holding up two fingers. Hal and Tennessee sat down on one of the benches and watched as Lay reached into a box filled with rice husks and brought out the precious block of ice that had been delivered earlier. She carefully wiped the ice clean, chopped pieces off, and dropped them into two glasses. The "chink, chink" of ice being chopped, the "clink" of the ice dropping into the glasses, and the fizz of the coke being poured were satisfying sounds that dispelled the threat of the day's rising heat. In all its simplicity, Lay's coke-stand represented luxury, a touch of exotica.

Though no older than ten, Lay handled the money they gave her with confidence, counting out their change. They sipped their drinks, and Hal pressed the cold glass against his forehead. Water pooled on his skin like dew, and he sighed with contentment.

Two small dogs skulked at the stand's periphery in hopes of scraps. The thin, squalid animals looked like ancient prototypes of modern domestic canines. "Dee-dee!" Lay scolded, and she kicked at the fleeing scavengers. Hal could not recall having observed a Vietnamese actually petting a dog. Instead, dogs were treated with indifference, and their ultimate fate, unlike the American pet cemetery, was as table fare.

A long procession of ducks approached them. An old man walked behind the entourage carrying a long stick that he used occasionally to reprimand or coax a wayward animal. There were perhaps sixty ducks strutting in peaceful, orderly file under the old man's stick. Hal and Tennessee nodded at the man as he passed, and he raised his hand and smiled.

"Where does he go with the ducks?" Hal asked Lay.

"Him come when men fini with rice," Lay replied.

"He comes to the rice paddies?"

Lay nodded. "Ducks, they eat rice."

"Ah, they eat the rice left after it's been cut," Hal said.

Lay nodded in affirmation, smiling.

Hal and Tennessee, safe from the glare of the sun, sipped their drinks. "I heard some weird noises last night," Hal told Tennessee.

"Yeah? Like what?"

"Oh, like something sneaking along the creek. That's what it sounded like. I came close to popping a flare."

"Probably just some pigs," Tennessee said. A week earlier the mortar squad on the hill had fired up what they thought was enemy movement, but the next morning they discovered they had decimated a herd of wild pigs.

"Yeah. Anyways, I didn't feel like hassling with the Hill."

"Yeah, man. Those idiots!"

"I don't know which is worse, fat-ass Martin or the cherry lieutenant."

A convoy of deuce-and-a-halves crammed with South Vietnamese troops passed through the village. The soldiers flashed two fingers in the peace sign, the universal greeting. Hal and Tennessee answered in kind, despite the contempt they felt for the South Vietnamese Army's willingness or ability to fight.

A jeep with two Vietnamese policemen pulled up at the stand. The Americans dubbed the white-uniformed Vietnamese police "white mice." Arrogant, superior opportunists, the "white mice" commonly represented all that was corrupt in the South Vietnamese government. The two officers took seats and ordered drinks. A motorcycle carrying two "cowboys" dressed in the stylish mix of military and civilian clothing also stopped. They, too, ordered drinks from Lay, and a lively, rapid conversation ensued amongst the Vietnamese.

"I suppose we'd better get back," Tennessee said at length.

"Yeah, it's about time for my shift," Hal agreed.

They walked back to the bridge. Sonny and Bo were sharing a joint while the Temptations blared a song from the tape-deck.

"We miss anything exciting?" Tennessee asked.

"Oh yeah, man," Sonny said, rolling his eyes. "I'm glad you dudes are back. I'm gonna go get me a cool drink at Lay's."

"Me too," Bo said. The two sauntered toward the village, thus effectually completing the changing of the guard.

"Wake me up when it's my watch," Tennessee said, and he descended into the relative cool of the bunker.

Hal leaned his M-16 against the sandbags and set his helmet beside it. They were supposed to wear their helmets while on duty, but it didn't make sense in this heat. The words "I'll get high with a little help from my friends" were inscribed on the helmet, and a metal peace symbol was attached to it. Hal lit a joint and tried to relax in the relentless, dusty heat. He considered the mail and hot meal they would be getting from headquarters. Once a week they got a hot meal from the battalion mess hall, which was a welcome change from their C-rations. More importantly, they received mail—that mystical gift that could bring joy or sorrow. Lately, for Hal, there had been more of the latter. His girlfriend had broken off their relationship after finding "someone who more closely shared her goals in life." His brother, who was involved in college campus anti-war demonstrations, wrote that Hal was "morally wrong to be fighting an unjust and indecent war." Mail call had become strange and sometimes painful, but like an addict, he was hooked on words from home. He longed for them as relief from the daily monotony and the nightly fear that his life had become.

A motorcycle bearing a family of five labored across the bridge, followed by a bus packed with passengers headed for Quin Nhon. Two boys rode on top of the bus amidst a mound of luggage. Hal wished that he was on that bus, riding on top where the two boys were sitting, roaring down the highway, the wind tearing at him, going someplace, anyplace, away from the bridge.

Hal sat facing west, toward the dark jungle-clad mountains. Rice paddies and dikes stretched into the distance, an ordered pattern broken here and there by clumps of trees that concealed farm houses and small hamlets. The valley's lush greenery stretched perhaps two miles to the west, to the darker green of the mountains—foothills, really, leading to the rugged mountains of the interior. Hal's attention was drawn to the white flickerings of butterflies. There were hundreds of them, flitting and bobbing with the light breeze. The more he looked around him the more he saw, thousands of them fluttering; a moving mosaic diminishing into the distance, part of some impetuous migration. It was amid these observations that he was startled by the sudden rush of a jet fighter sweeping by overhead. The fighter raced westward toward the mountains, banked, then dove and fired a rocket. A resounding explosion shattered the lazy day, and Hal watched a black cone of smoke rise from the distant paddies. Another jet screamed overhead and traced the path of the first, fired a rocket, and a second explosion rent the day. Hal could see the villagers in their paddies, standing frozen, tiny in the distance, tools suspended in their hands, watching the jets. The planes circled and made another pass. Flying in low, they fired another round of rockets. Banking again, the jets whistled back past Hal and were gone, leaving the silenced fields and the four black plumes of smoke.

"What the hell goes on?" Tennessee cried, as he emerged from the bunker.

"Damned if I know," Hal said. They looked out at the fields and watched the smoke slowly dissipate. Gradually, the workers began to move again, and the landscape regained the semblance of normalcy. Hal knew they would never learn what had just happened. Whether the jets had attacked an NVA or Viet Cong unit, or it was merely a case of two fly-boys shooting up a water buffalo, was anybody's guess.

Tennessee retreated once again into the bunker, and the day droned on. After the younger village children had gotten out of school, they began to filter down to the bridge for what had become a daily ritual. First, Bo "treated" the water. He carried a hand-grenade to the center of the bridge, pulled the pin, and dropped it into the pool below. A muffled explosion created a geyser of water, and several small fish floated belly-up in the muddy pool. This precaution served to control the leech population.

The creek originated in the mountains to the west and irrigated the fields through which it ran before reaching the bridge. It was narrow enough to jump across in most places, but at the bridge it widened into a large pool. The water was always muddy and smelled foul. The human feces with which the Vietnamese fertilized their rice paddies seemed infinitely more filthy than the cow manure used in the fields of home, and the Americans were more than a little squeamish about getting into water that flowed through such terrain. However, heat and boredom will defeat the loftiest of moral standards.

Bo fetched the Army-issue air mattresses from the bunker, and he and Hal joined the laughing gaggle of kids that raced down the bank to the edge of the swimming hole. Clothes were quickly stripped away and the brown slender bodies slithered into the water, splashing, leaping and screaming. Great battles ensued, where the children, manning the air mattress battleships, were ruthlessly stalked and flung into the water by the piratical GIs.

The pandemonium was momentarily hushed when a woman's scolding voice broke upon them in rapid Vietnamese. A woman from the village stood on the bridge glaring down at them. One of the boys hurriedly dressed while the lady, reminding Hal of his mother when he had neglected a chore, stood in stern silence with hands on hips. Play broke out afresh after they departed.

A convoy ground across the bridge overhead, and from his air mattress Hal watched the dusty soldiers pass. Some of them noticed him floating in the water and flashed the peace sign, a look of envy on their grimy faces. Hal returned the peace signs like magnanimous royalty.

Bo had just dressed and climbed up the bank when he reappeared and hissed in alarm, "Here comes Martin!"

"Lifer!" Hal told the kids with urgency. "Quick! Out of sight. Lifer come!"

A tidal wave of bodies lunged across the water toward the bridge. The children gathered around Hal in a knot inside the mouth of the culvert just as a jeep pulled up onto the bridge above them.

Hal could hear Sergeant Martin's gruff voice and the more subdued voices of Sonny and Bo as they unloaded the jeep.

Hal stiffened when he heard sergeant Martin ask, "Where's Henley?"

"In the village, I guess," Sonny answered a bit weakly.

"You guess? Don't you know?"

"He's in the village, Sergeant!" Sonny replied, now with enough of a smart-ass tone to sound convincing.

Hal observed with horror the wealth of incriminating evidence that had been left on display—the piles of clothes at the water's edge and, worst of all, an air mattress floating in the middle of the pool. Hal looked down at his co-conspirators. Their eyes were wide and alert to danger.

"What the hell is he doing in the village? He got a girlfriend or something?"

"He just went for a coke."

"You guys must think you're on vacation or something. I want your asses here at your post! At all times!"

There was a little splash, and Sergeant Martin's cigar-butt bobbed like a smoldering turd on the water's surface. It had missed the air mattress by inches. Hal could hear some threat about withholding their mail and chow, and then it was silent. It was a moment before he realized the jeep had continued across the bridge toward the Hill. Its engine sound finally diminished in the distance.

Able to breathe normally again, Hal, in a suddenly officious voice, ordered the kids, "Come on now, dee-dee!"

As if released from a stupor, the children dashed across the pool to their clothes, accepting the fickle nature of the Americans' emotions. They dressed quickly and scattered like rabbits back toward the village, shouting, "Lifah! Lifah! Lifah!"

Hal gathered his composure as he dressed. Maybe he had some mail, a letter from home. And he was starving, just thinking about a good hot meal. "Fucking lifers," he mumbled, as he climbed up out of the creek.

II

"Man, that was a close one," said Sonny.

"Yeah. Fuck Martin," Hal said. "I get any mail?"

"Not for us," Sonny answered, "just for those two," and he nodded toward Bo and Tennessee, who were sitting on sandbags reading their letters.

Hal observed with envy their total absorption in the letters from home. "What's for supper? he asked Sonny, who was peering into the two o.d.-green marmite cans.

"Looks like tuna casserole and green beans," Sonny answered, and they made faces at each other.

"Well, it beats C-rations, anyways," Hal said, and they dished themselves healthy portions.

"There's chocolate cake for desert," Sonny said.

"Hey, now you're talking," Hal said. "Hey, you guys had better come and get some while you can."

Bo and Tennessee looked up and gave vague nods, but returned to their letters. Only when they had completed a thorough first reading did they join Hal and Sonny for supper.

"My sister had her baby," Bo said. "I'm an uncle!"

"With all the brothers and sisters you got, you'd better get used to it," Sonny said.

"What's the news?" Hal asked Tennessee.

"Oh, nothing much. Same old shit."

Hal could understand the note of sadness. It was the same old shit, but they were missing it. Things were happening back home, back in the World, but they weren't part of it. They weren't in the World anymore.

The dreaded heat was retreating, and it felt comfortable despite the few mosquitoes that were beginning to appear. Kids, too, began to drift toward the bridge from the village: Tim and Tuan; Lay and her best friend Lin; and smaller kids like Mao and Chin. It seemed inconceivable that such a small village could produce so many children. Indeed, wherever Hal went, it was the children that he noticed, a flood of them, intelligent, full of fun and mischief, much like children anywhere, their enthusiasm for life unblunted by the war that raged around them.

The mess hall always sent a full thermos of food, much more than the four of them could eat. Thus, the children habitually came to the bridge for a share of the hot meals.

"You kids line up," Sonny told them, trying to create order out of the gaggle of small bodies gathered around Bo, who was spooning food into the frantically beckoning bowls. When their bowls had been filled, the kids shyly scampered back to the village to eat the exotic American food.

"Man, these people don't know what a line is," Sonny declared, after the food had been doled out and the children had dispersed.

"That's a fact," Tennessee agreed. "I'd hate to be a traffic cop over here."

They were sitting on the bunker eating cake and drinking "real" coffee.

"Man, this is the best cake I ever ate," exclaimed Hal.

"Amen, brother," Sonny agreed.

"Even better than pound cake," Bo said, referring to the C-ration fare that was a favorite.

"We'd better close the bridge," Sonny said, after they had finished their cake. Daylight was fading, and it would soon be dark.

They dragged the strands of concertina wire across the road and then checked the claymore mines that were emplaced around the perimeter. The claymore was a deadly device, convex-shaped, filled with hundreds of steel b-bs, and backed with C-4 explosive. A wire led from each mine to the bunker, where electronic triggering devices were arrayed. They had heard the horror stories of claymores being mysteriously turned around and GIs unwittingly firing them on their own positions. Besides the claymores, their M-16 rifles, hand grenades, illumination flares, and an M-60 machine-gun comprised their defensive weapons.

Sonny turned the radio on and waited for the evening radio schedule with the Hill. The only non-draftee among the four, Sonny had recently received his sergeant stripe and was officially in charge of the bridge. Bo washed out the marmite cans, and the others policed the area while it was still light enough to see. They gravitated toward the radio to listen when they heard the call, *"Eagle-two, this is Eagle-one, over."*

They listened to Cathcart from Bridge Eleven answer the call from the Hill: *"Eagle-one, this is Eagle-two. I read you loud and clear, over."*

"Eagle-two, Eagle-one. Roger, I read you loud and clear. Be extra-vigilant tonight down there, over."

"Roger, roger."

Hal could hear the weariness in Cathcart's reply and could imagine him rolling his eyes, exchanging profanities with Day.

"Break, Eagle-three, this is Eagle-one, over."

"Eagle-one, this is Eagle-three. I read you loud and clear," Sonny answered.

"*Eagle-three, Eagle-one. Roger, I read you loud and clear. Keep your eyes and ears open tonight, over.*"

"Roger, roger, over," Sonny replied.

"Oh, roger on that," Tennessee said. "Shit."

"*Eagle-one out.*"

"Eagle-three out." Sonny set the microphone down. "And have a nice day."

Sonny pulled out his sack of Bombers and lit one. The others did likewise, and they sat on the sandbags smoking and watching the stars gain prominence in the darkening sky.

"I wonder what's going on back in the World tonight," Sonny said.

"Your girl's getting banged right now," Bo said.

"Yeah," Sonny replied, "and your favorite milk-cow's getting banged, too."

"Nah, she'll wait for me," Bo said amid laughter.

"Sounds like the place is going nuts," Tennessee said. "There's all kinds of college campus anti-war demonstrations going on. Hell, my *father* even says we shouldn't be here! That's a switch. He said he was so proud when I left."

"My brother says we're morally wrong to be over here," Hal said.

"That's heavy," said Sonny.

"Shit, it's like we're a bunch of fuck-ups all of a sudden," Tennessee said. "I don't get it."

"I don't see what they expect," Bo said. "We're here. We can't just up and leave."

"We pull out now and what happens to the Vietnamese that depend on us, like this village here?" asked Hal.

"We're pulling out, though," said Sonny. "Vietnamization, man. It amounts to the same shit."

"What a crock," Tennessee said. "We could win this war in a month if we were allowed to fight it. Instead we're sitting here on our asses. Fucking targets, is all *we* are."

"Same old shit," Hal said, fishing a harmonica out of his shirt pocket. "All I know is, I've got ninety-six days and a wake-up, and I'm out of here."

"A two digit midget. Damn!" Bo said.

"That's me." Hal blew into the harmonica to clear the reeds, and then he began playing a tune.

"I'll be right behind you, man," Tennessee said. "Then the Army can kiss my ass!"

"Oh, you'll miss Martin," Bo said.

"That's one son of a bitch I won't miss."

"At least we're not on the Hill," said Sonny.

"Yeah, Mimms says they're having inspections!" Tennessee said.

"No shit?" said Hal, lowering his harmonica in mid-song.

"That's Lieutenant Edmond's idea," Sonny said.

"Those poor fuckers!"

"I guess they figure we got nothing better to do," Bo said.

"Too much of that shit ain't healthy," Tennessee said.

"Mimms says there was another fragging at English a couple of nights ago—the first-sergeant of Headquarters Company."

"They get him?"

"Nah, just a few frag wounds in his ass."

"They know who did it?"

"I don't think so. I hear he's transferring to another unit, though. It must have scared the shit out of him!"

"I guess."

Though sitting only a few feet apart, they were now disembodied voices in the darkness, marked only by the glow of their joints. "You got first watch, Hal," Sonny said.

"Okay," Hal replied. They rotated watches every week, and now it was Hal's turn for the coveted first watch.

While the others prepared for sleep, Hal arranged the flashlight and illumination flares in front of him. He lay his M-16 on the sandbags next to his helmet and extra clips of ammunition.

Once the others had turned in, the whole character of the night changed. Gone was the easy camaraderie of a few minutes ago. Hal was suddenly plunged into a lonely vigil, marooned on a tiny sandbag island in a vast sea of darkness.

At LZ English, the brigade base camp, guard duty was very different from here. Hal thought of the bunker parties, of the huge bamboo pipe with four stems extending from it. The pipe held three ounces of marijuana and could only be lit with a piece of C-4. Once lit, it burned into the night, emitting a campfire glow. But here there were no bunker parties. Instead, Hal sat bird-like, straining to hear beyond the peeping of frogs and the insect sounds that arose from the black stillness.

Overhead, an occasional meteorite streaked across the canopy of stars. He had never seen so many falling stars as frequented these skies, but then perhaps suburbia of upstate New York wasn't optimum for star-gazing. It seemed that he'd never had the time to really think before. But here, in the solitude of night, his mind traveled to many places and times: past, present, and future.

He recalled another starry night nine months earlier: sitting on his duffel bag, a nineteen year old kid amid two hundred other young soldiers at Fort Lewis, Washington, waiting to fly to war; the subdued rustle of uncertainty as they shifted and exchanged nervous chatter. He remembered his last look at the United States of America after they had finally taken off from McCord Air Force Base: Mount Ranier's peak thrusting skyward, almost melting into the misty blue of the early morning--a quiet farewell. They had flown on a commercial jet airliner, complete with stewardesses—a first indication of the incongruity of the war that awaited him.

Hal's first view of Vietnam was of a spectacular coastline, the brilliant white beach bracketed by the lush green of vegetation inland and the light aqua water seaward, transforming in gradations to the deep blue of the South China Sea. The plane landed at Cam Rahn Bay, and a blast of hot air greeted him as he disembarked.

They were herded into formations, then onto buses with wire mesh covering the windows-- a precaution against grenades, they were told. The buses lumbered across barren sand and down concertina-wire corridors, through the desolation of the huge US installation. Hal remembered a guy from New York City remarking, "I thought we were flying to Vietnam. Hell, we're in Jersey!"

Processing and indoctrination followed. They were cautioned about booby traps and venereal disease; were told about an island where GIs who had contracted incurable strains of VD were sent to live in isolated quarantine. Rosters; roll-calls; and back on the buses. Hal boarded a C-130 for the flight north to Quin Nhon and then on to Phu Cat, where more processing and indoctrination awaited.

The final leg of the journey, a fifty-mile truck ride to LZ English, gave Hal his first close look at the country. It was the monsoon season, and a steady drizzle fell from an opaque, mist-laden sky. The traffic-clogged highway passed through a heavily populated countryside dominated by mud and water. It was all so new, so absolutely foreign, that Hal's eyes bugged in an attempt to take it all in: rice paddies laid out in geometric precision; water buffalo at work in the fields; palm trees; banana trees; temples and monks in yellow robes; the dark line of mountains beckoning to the west; buses, motorcycles, and lambrettas freighted with passengers and a wide array of goods; truckloads of Vietnamese soldiers going south. And overlying all this was the Vietnamese populace: Men and women in conical hats laboring in the rice paddies or squatting alongside the highway; a vast humanity crowded into cities, villages, and hamlets that buzzed with commerce and were rife with smells from fish markets and food stalls.

Nine months had intervened since that truck ride north. Hal hadn't encountered the anticipated battles but, instead, had endured and endless succession of days heavy with boredom punctuated by the unexpected moments of terror in the form of mortar attacks, booby traps, or sniper fire. He had lost friends, not on the field of battle, but from cleverly-laid traps and pathetic accidents: Burgess killed by a mortar round; Schmidt's foot blown off by a land mine; Garcia shot in the gut when White's rifle accidentally discharged; Cox's hand grievously injured by a malfunctioning smoke grenade. The soldiers had begun to question the judgment of their superiors. They were prevented from confronting their enemy or, conversely, were wasted on missions that accomplished little if anything. The war of attrition had lost validity, and the soldiers had become sullen and defiant. They counted the days until they would board the Freedom Bird for home.

Hal often consulted his personal calendar, ticking each day off in anticipation of his return. There was a rising grain of fear, however, an undefined anxiety that clouded his thoughts of the future. He didn't know what to expect. He knew there would be no parades for the returning warriors, and more, he had come to ponder an air of hostility, if not from his friends and family, then from the faceless mass of society. He thought of the bus ride home, surrounded by people not wearing uniforms to define them, leading tidy unsullied lives. He thought about seeing Pam again. He hadn't really expected her to wait for him, had he? He'd been gone for almost two years, and they had gone steady just their senior year of high school. That seemed eons ago. Hal didn't know what to think. He suspected that he was afraid to confront his emotions. He was struggling to think like a man and not like the boy he once was, the last time he'd seen Mount Ranier.

He slapped a mosquito, idly wondering if it carried malaria. They were ordered to take their anti-malaria tablets regularly, and, just as with the mandate to avoid drinking village water, it was an order they routinely ignored. Contracting malaria would result in a free ticket home--not an unattractive prognosis. However, all attempts at disease had proved fruitless.

Hal shifted back against the sandbags but then shot straight up when he heard a splash in the creek. The frogs were suddenly quiet, like someone had flicked a switch. He held his breath and listened, trying to penetrate the background whisperings of crickets. There, again, he heard a splash; not the hollow plunk of a frog or reptile, but the whoosh of a large body moving through the water. Hal knew there was a wide variety of strange animals in this country, but he'd never seen anything much bigger than a lizard. He couldn't picture what creature might be walking in the creek. He imagined, instead, the stealthy approach of a Viet Cong sapper, dressed in black and armed with explosives. Stare as he might, however, he failed to distinguish any shapes or movements in the blackness.

Minutes passed. Hal strained to pick up any sound. He could hear water noises, but as a very remote, faint roaring, as if the creek conducted the sounds of its raucous birth from the distant mountains. It was unimaginable that the miasmal seepage of brown water flowing under the bridge could rouse a hint of its passing.

Surely a VC would be more careful, more sly, and more deadly than to splash the water. Hal knew though, that the creek was the perfect approach for a sapper. A wise aggressor would avoid the open fields. He would utilize the vegetation along the shallow banks of the creek for concealment and make a patient, determined advance.

More minutes passed, and Hal was breathing normally again, ready to believe it was an animal after all. He looked down at the glow from his watch and was pleased to see only fifteen minutes of his shift remained.

Tennessee was difficult to wake up, and getting him out of bed was becoming harder over time. Hal had to start the process of awaking him a little earlier each night. With ten minutes left on the clock he groped his way down into the bunker and, with his hand over the lens, turned the flashlight on. The bunker's interior was like a rock cavern in the dim light. He found Tennessee curled up in the corner. "Tennessee," he hissed, bending over the dark form and prodding it. When there was no reaction he shook him again. "Tennessee!"

"Yeah, okay," Tennessee responded, but too vaguely to satisfy Hal.

"Tennessee. Your watch."

"What? Okay."

"You're awake?"

"Yeah, yeah, I'll be right there."

"Okay," Hal said, and he went back outside. When five minutes had elapsed he went back into the bunker. Tennessee was once again in the fetal position. "Tennessee!" Hal said with a more violent prod. "Tennessee!"

"What? What?" Tennessee's head came up.

"Get up! It's your watch, man."

"Yeah, okay," Tennessee replied, but his head went back down.

"Get up, dammit!" Again Hal prodded.

This time Tennessee sat up and began rubbing his eyes.

"It's your watch," Hal told him.

"Yeah, okay," Tennessee said, yawning.

Hal went back outside and waited five more minutes. When he went back inside Tennessee was sitting up, but he hadn't put his boots on yet. "Come on, man. It's your watch, so let's go."

"Okay, I'm coming," Tennessee said, and he bent to the task pulling on his boots--an encouraging sign.

A couple of minutes later Tennessee finally emerged from the bunker, yawning and stretching. He sat down next to Hal. "Man, it's dark as hell." he said.

"Tell me about it." Hal sat with him for a few minutes to be sure he was really awake. One of the worst of sins was to fall asleep on guard duty.

"Anything happening?" Tennessee asked.

"There were a couple of splashes in the creek," Hal said. "That was about a half hour ago, though. It's been quiet since then. It must have been some animal."

"Yeah. Probably a pig."

"Yeah, must be." Hal finally rose and groped his way into the bunker and to the corner that Tennessee had vacated. He took his boots off and lay down on the sandbags, not caring about the dirt, suddenly very tired.

III

Daylight filtered through the bunker's doorway and gun-ports when Hal awoke. Inches from his head, a gecko lizard clung to the sandbags that formed the wall. The small tan creature was poised, immobile, on its padded, knobby toes that enabled it to climb vertical surfaces. The villagers considered geckos to be omens of good luck and allowed them to reside in their homes unmolested. At night geckos commonly lurked near lights, where they feasted on the insects drawn into the glow. Hal raised a hand, and the gecko's over-sized head shifted at the movement. Its large eyes goggled at the finger Hal slowly extended in an attempt to pet him. With a sudden move of surprising speed, the lizard whipped around and scuttled out of sight into the cracks between the sandbags.

Hal raised his head and peered into the gloom of the basement dwelling. Sonny was in the hammock he had purchased in the village, and Tennessee was snoring across from him on the opposite sandbag bench. The only furnishings that graced the dwelling were a table fashioned out of a piece of plywood set on sandbags and ammo boxes that served as chairs and foot-lockers. Rubbing his face, Hal felt the grit of dirt on his skin. He dragged his boots up from the floor, making a little cloud of disturbance in the dust. *One less wake-up.* The thought made all else more tolerable.

Bo was on duty, watching the sunrise and smoking a bomber.

"Hey, Bo."

"Hey, Bo." They both laughed at the old greeting.

Bo Doyle was from Tyus, Georgia, a self-avowed cow-fucker, and he didn't give a hoot about the city boys' thoughts on the subject. Hal sat down next to him, and they smoked, looking to the crimson sky in the east. "Another day." Hal mouthed the bleak thought and coughed a cloud of smoke.

"At least we're not on the Hill," Bo said. "I'm mighty glad I don't have to look at Martin every morning."

"Him or the lieutenant."

"Next they'll be having morning formations up there!"

"And PT."

"Yeah, I'd like to see Martin doing PT," Bo said, and laughed.

"I bet he can't even do a push-up."

Bo flicked the remnant of his joint onto the ground. "Recon we'd better get the gate."

They walked to the bridge and dragged the wire fences off to the side of the road. "Open for business," Bo said.

"Yeah. Airborne." The thought of another hot day of sitting in the dust cloud of the highway was depressing.

Bo disappeared into the bunker for a nap, and Hal heated some water for coffee. He put his Grand Funk Railroad tape into the road-weary tape-deck and cranked up the volume. He looked again to the east, where the scrubby hills robbed any view of the ocean. He often dreamed of climbing those hills to see what the other side looked like. The ocean couldn't be very far. He was sure there was a glorious white sandy beach just over those hills, and yet it might as well be in another country. He could only look out at the surrounding countryside and wonder what it would be like, sitting on top of one of the hills, bathed in sea-breeze and looking out at the expansive sweep of the ocean; that, or to be sitting in one of the palm-grove islands that dotted the rice paddies, enjoying the cool shade and the tranquil clucking of chickens.

"Hey man, all's well?" Tennessee asked, as he stepped out into the sunlight.

"All is fucking lovely," Hal replied.

"It's going to be a hot one today," said Tennessee, stretching.

"Yeah, I'm already starting to sweat." Hal fired another bomber, more from habit than for effect. He'd been smoking so much pot that he wasn't even sure if he got stoned anymore. It seemed more to contribute to an inherent weariness.

The cattle from the village, driven by the three boys, clomped past them and across the bridge. Hal and Tennessee waved to them as they passed. The boys smiled, and one said something in Vietnamese, making the others laugh. Tennessee rose up and made a lunge as if to chase them, and the boys screamed with delight and ran across the bridge.

An old French truck piled high with coconuts rattled past, making the wooden planks rumble as it crossed the bridge. A lazy cloud of dust hung in its wake, and Hal could taste the red dirt as it passed over them.

"Hey, baby," cried Sonny. "I can't sleep with that honkey music blaring away out here! Put the Temptations on, man."

"It's the guru of Motown," said Hal. He changed tapes, and Sonny gyrated to the music. "What's got you in such a good mood today?" Hal asked.

"What's got me in such a good mood? I'll tell you, man," Sonny said, doing a twirl. "I'm one day closer to being back in the World, Man."

"Congratulations," Tennessee said.

"Looks like a jeep coming," Hal said, looking up the highway.

They turned to watch the approaching vehicle. "Looks like it's from the Hill," Sonny said, but they relaxed when they saw it held but a lone figure at the wheel.

The jeep clattered across the bridge and screeched to a halt beside the bunker.

"They're letting you out all by yourself" Sonny asked. "Damn, Mimms, you got it knocked!"

"Where's Martin?" asked Hal.

"There's a big project up on the Hill," Mimms said, his lips tight in a grimace. "We're rebuilding the perimeter."

"What?" Tennessee said in disbelief.

"That's right," Mimms said, "the whole damn thing!"

"Oh man, that should keep you guys busy for awhile," Sonny said with a laugh.

"Yeah. "Mimms spit bitterly. "I have to pick up sandbags. The lieutenant wants to rebuild a couple of the bunkers, too. Damn, we're so short-handed we barely have enough guys to pull guard duty, and now this shit!"

"You poor fuckers," said Tennessee, laughing uproariously.

They loaded the marmite cans and coffee thermos into the jeep for the return trip to the battalion mess hall.

"You guys just don't know how to live right up there," Sonny said.

"Very funny. I can see you guys are full of sympathy," Mimms replied. "I'd better go. Martin is hot to get the sandbags. See you assholes later." He pulled the jeep back onto the road and sped off toward LZ English.

"Those poor fuckers," Hal said.

Bo laughed. "Boy, Mimms was sure pissed off."

"That new lieutenant is a fuck-up," Sonny said.

"I'm sure glad we aren't up there," Hal said.

"We aren't entirely safe," Sonny said. "They could still pull some shit."

"Like what?"" asked Tennessee.

"Damned if I know for sure. They could dream something up, though."

They fell silent, considering the means available to the Hill to impose itself upon their lives.

"Fuck it," Bo said. "Let's play some cards."

"Might as well," agreed Tennessee.

"Okay, man," said Sonny, "I'll give you guys a chance to get even."

Tennessee, Bo and Sonny went into the bunker to set up the card table and begin another card marathon, one of their chief entertainments.

Hal arranged the guard seat-- two ammo boxes with sandbags set on top-- and placed his accessories around him: M-16; steel helmet; web-gear; and tape-deck. One never knew when a Lieutenant-Colonel might be in one of the convoys, looking for trouble. It was better to be prepared, if not exactly militarily correct. Sweating freely now, Hal took his shirt off and put the Rolling Stones into the tape-deck.

Oaths erupted from inside the bunker as the card game heated up. Hal could hear Tennessee yelling, "You lucky sucker!" The outburst generated raucous laughter. Hal leaned back and closed his eyes against the glare of the sun. Rivulets of sweat dripped off his chin and ran down his body.

Traffic increased, and the air became a haze of dust. A convoy, led by an MP jeep, began its relentless march across the bridge. Hal's two fingers rose and fell in answer to the peace signs the soldiers flashed from the backs of deuce-and-a-halves, almost like he was saluting. APCs, with three or four soldiers riding on top, ground past, churning a billowing cloud of dust. A big flat-bed carrying heavy machinery passed, followed by tanks, and the dust got so thick that Hal put his shirt back on and tied a bandana over his mouth so he could breathe. He plugged the ear phones into the tape-deck so he could hear the music above the chaos.

When the convoy had finally passed, Hal lowered the bandana. He could feel the dirt sticking to his wet skin and coating his hair. The music played on, oblivious to the elements.

Tennessee eventually emerged from the bunker to relieve him. Hal washed his face and doused his hair. The cool water flowing over him felt very good. He drank deeply and then ducked into the bunker. Here it was cooler, though not entirely free from the dust storm. Bo was asleep, and Sonny was in his hammock reading.

"Hot out there?" Sonny asked.

"Hot as shit," Hal answered. "I'm soaking wet from sweat." He found his book, a Western, and lay down to read. He was soon transported to another world, another time. Yet, this other world, where Apaches were pursued through sand-clogged arroyos, was plagued by the same heat and dust. There seemed to be no escape from the dust.

Hal didn't know how long he'd been asleep, but he was aroused by the stirring of Bo and Sonny as they struggled with their gear and scrambled for the bunker's door. "What's up?"" he asked.

"Mimms is back with our rations," Sonny answered.

Hal jumped up and joined the others gathered around the jeep. The cases of C-rations were unloaded and immediately rifled, each of them grabbing for coveted meals. The meals were rated by popularity. Beans and Franks, with its accompanying pound cake, was the top prize. Other meals, such as Spaghetti, were also highly esteemed. Beef Stew and Ham and Eggs were met with less favor, while Spiced Beef, which nobody liked, occupied the lowest rank. The frenzy, accomplished by practiced hands, was short-lived, and each had his booty gathered beside him. Mimms handed out their cigarette rations. They were each allotted two cartons a week. Although none of them smoked, they accepted the cigarettes avidly. The cartons of American cigarettes were hot items on the extensive Vietnamese black market, and were thus good bartering material.

"What's the story on the dead gooks on the road?" Mimms asked.

"What dead gooks?"" Sonny asked.

"Well, there's three dead gooks laying alongside the road just the other side of the village," Mimms said.

"It's the first we heard about it."

"They weren't there when I went by this morning, but they're there now."

"No shit? Wow, man, that's weird," Tennessee said. "Nobody said anything to us about it."

"I'd better get these up to the Hill," Mimms said, nodding at the sandbags piled in the back of the jeep.

"Later, man," Sonny said, and they watched Mimms drive across the bridge.

"Maybe we'd better check out these dead gooks," Sonny added, as they gathered up their C-rations and cigarettes.

"Where'd they come from?" asked Bo.

"How should I know?""Sonny replied. "Let's check it out."

They carried their goods into their lair and, leaving Tennessee to man the bridge, set out toward the village.

A row of trees about one hundred yards from the bridge delineated the village. From there, a cluster of houses fronted the road. Each yard was fenced with bamboo or barbed-wire in order to confine livestock. Children, on bicycles and on foot, were returning home from school. Looking scrubbed and preened, they jumped and ran, singing songs. The boys wore white shirts and checkered shorts, and the girls wore white shirts and loose-fitting pants, white, pink, or black in color.

"VC! VC!"" Lay and Lin cried, running up to them, their eyes wide with excitement.

"Dead VC?" asked Sonny. "Where?"

"We show you," the girls cried, leading them now to the opposite end of the village.

A few boys were loitering near the three bodies that lay in the grass beside the road. Tim and Tuan saw their approach and ran to them. "Dead VC!" Tuan called, unable to disguise his agitation. He talked sharply to Lay, his younger sister, and the girls backed off a few paces.

"How they dead?" asked Sonny.

"From there," Tim replied, pointing to the hills to the south.

"Who killed the VC?" Sonny asked them.

"Arvin kill VC, last night," said Tim, using the popularized term for ARVN, the Army of the Republic of Vietnam.

"They got them in an ambush last night?" Sonny asked them.

The boys nodded. The children moved away as the soldiers reached the corpses, forming a little knot and whispering excitedly as they watched the Americans.

All three bodies were lying face-up, staring mindlessly at the sky. One was bound, hands and feet, to the pole he had been carried out on, like a safari trophy.

"I can't believe we didn't hear anything," Hal said.

"We might not if they were on the other side of the hills," Bo said.

"I thought I heard some explosions," Sonny said. "They could have come from over there."

They often heard gun-fire and the distant clamor of artillery at night, but in the randomness of the war such instances were but mild curiosities, rarely to be explained.

Two of the bodies were clad in the khaki of NVA soldiers, pants tightly rolled up into shorts. The other body wore the black pajamas of the peasant. Their clothing was ruffled and open, where the South Vietnamese soldiers had pilfered their belongings. They wore belts with empty ammo-pouches, the flaps splayed open. The corpses looked like hurricane victims.

"They had the shit shot out of them," Sonny said.

"Yeah," Hal replied quietly, as they looked down at the scene of carnage.

The faces of the dead men were unblemished, almost peaceful. The skin was pale and shiny, like plastic, and the eyes had a vacant glow, like glass. The bodies were ravaged. The one in black pajamas was missing both legs, and each pant-leg was tied in a knot. They all had shrapnel wounds, ranging from the size of a dime to gaping, fist-sized holes.

"Looks like claymores," Sonny said.

"They must have had an ambush set up on a trail," said Hal.

The NVA that was bound had one side of his skull blown off. If you looked from one side, he appeared perfectly normal. But if you looked at the other side, there was a section of the skull above the ear that was missing, like his head had been cross-sectioned in order to display the brain.

"Him from here," Tuan said, pointing to the man in black.

"You know him?" asked Sonny.

"Yes! Yes!" Tuan and Tim replied.

"He's from this village?" Hal asked them.

"No, not this village. Not far," Tim said, and he pointed up the road toward Bong Son.

Hal looked down upon this native son, so young like all of them. The body appeared tiny in death, and Hal suddenly felt the vulnerability of being so stripped of life, to lay naked before the eyes of strangers.

A lambretta approaching from Bong Son slowed and pulled off the road next to the bodies. Two teenage boys and an old lady got out. The old lady was crying.

"Family him," Tuan said, nodding to the body in black. The onlookers instinctively backed away a few paces, shuffling in silence with the downcast eyes of mourners.

The two boys looked like they could be younger brothers of the dead man. They walked over to the body and stood looking down at it. The old lady followed them, and her crying erupted into shrieks when she saw the body. The boys went to her and held both her arms, supporting her sagging body. Her pinched, wrinkled face was contorted in grief, lips pulled back to expose teeth blackened from chewing beetle leaves. They gently guided her back to the vehicle and sat her down on the tail-gate. Taking a blanket from behind the lady, they walked back to the body. They spread the blanket on the ground, lifted the body onto it, and carefully carried the litter back to the waiting lambretta. The lady's crying rose again as they drew near. Her hands grabbed at the blanket as it was slid into the back of the lambretta. She was saying something over and over again, like a religious chant of ecstasy. The two boys were holding her again, talking to her. Hal looked down at the children standing beside him. They, too, were crying. The lady insisted on riding in back with the body, and the boys finally relented and helped her inside. The boys then looked over at the Americans for the first time, holding them with a brief gaze through slits that revealed no emotion. One of the boys got into the back with the old lady, while the other started the engine. As the lambretta pulled away the wailing increased, and the Americans stood as if rooted, listening to the cries recede down the highway.

Hal felt awkward, as though he'd been implicated by the withering glare of the two boys.

"What about these two?" Sonny finally asked, indicating the remaining two bodies.

The boys shrugged. "Them from far away," Tuan said.

"If nobody comes for them, what happens to them?" Hal asked.

"People from village bury them," Tuan replied, pointing off to the side of the road.

"That would be a hell of a note," Bo said, "getting planted alongside a highway."

There was a strong stench beginning to arise from the corpses that made them eager to quit the site. The three GIs walked back to the village with the kids dancing around them. "You come to my house," Lay told them.

"It's okay?" Hal asked.

"Yes, okay," Lay said. "You have a coca-cola."

They followed Lay through a gate and across a spotlessly clean bare-dirt yard to the front porch of her house. "You wait," she told them, and she went inside.

Trees spread above them in a canopy that blanketed the yard in shadows. The stucco house was a robin-egg blue color with a red tile roof. It was of the French villa style, with a wide front porch supported by four square pillars. On each side of the front door was a smaller door, and all were open to the dark interior. The wooden window-shutters were also open, maximizing circulation during the heat of the day. Two little girls came out onto the front porch to look at the Americans.

"It's sure nice to be out of the sun," Said Sonny.

"No kidding," Hal agreed. They had their shirts off, and their bodies glistened with sweat.

Lay came back out onto the porch with her mother, a handsome lady with a wise look in her eyes. She held a baby, its fat naked legs straddling her hip. She smiled at them and nodded and then said something to Lay.

"Come," Lay said, and she led them around to the back of the house. Here there was also a porch, and several chairs were arranged on it. Lay directed each guest to a chair and went inside the back door. The two little girls ventured onto the porch, shy but fascinated.

"Hi!" Bo said to the girls, smiling and nodding.

The girls' eyes widened, and they stared fixedly at the Americans.

Lay, the immaculate hostess, carried a tray with three glasses of coke. Ice tinkled against glass as she lowered the tray, offering the drinks.

They thanked her in turn, and each took a deep sip of the cooling liquid. The children laughed at their expressions, and the soldiers laughed, too.

A few red chickens, most of them missing feathers around the neck and breast, pecked at the dirt around the porch. Two pigs squabbled over some scrap, squealing and sprinting with a surprising speed, given their awkward build. Their backs swayed so that their bellies, supported by short, stubby legs, almost touched the ground.

Through the trees they could see the rice paddies, appearing to be endless from their restricted view. A breeze from the valley rustled the leaves around them.

Lay returned with Tuan. They had changed from their school clothes into their more rustic country apparel.

"You hot?" asked Tuan, laughing as he often did at the Americans' habit of sweating. Tuan was dry and unsullied, in contrast to the grimy, sodden appearance of the three soldiers.

"It feels real nice here now, Tuan," said Hal. Indeed, surrounded by war, the pastoral tranquility of life in the village seemed miraculous.

"You beaucoup hot," Tuan replied, and he sat down beside Hal.

Lay's mother came out onto the porch. She shifted the baby to her lap as she sat down at a table with chairs gathered around it, apparently where the family ate meals. She didn't speak any English and so depended upon her children to tell her what was being said. She lifted the baby with a sudden exclamation. Grabbing the towel that was draped over her shoulder, she dabbed and scrubbed at the baby's bare butt, scolding with a loud but good-natured voice. The two little girls rushed over to her side and laughed into their brother's eyes. Encouraged, the baby made a little fist and waved his arm up and down. The girls caressed his hands and cheeks. Sensing the limelight of attention, the baby became more animated. His fat face widened into an expanse of gums, revealing three teeth that stood out like little tusks. He screeched and bounced up and down, and they all laughed at the crazed antics.

Tuan turned to Hal. "How," he said, not able to pronounce the American name quite correctly. "You play?" Tuan made a blowing motion into his hands, mimicking a harmonica.

"I don't know," Hal replied, shuffling his feet.

"You play, yes," Lay pleaded.

"Okay," Hal relented. He took the harmonica from his pocket and blew a few tentative notes that brought laughter from his captive audience. He played *Old McDonald,* and Sonny and Bo started singing. The two warmed to the song, covering the full array of barnyard animals before they were done.

"Here, you try it," Hal told Tuan, handing him the harmonica.

Tuan blew into the instrument, producing a conglomeration of sounds that brought laughter from the others.

"Here, I show you," said Hal, and he took the harmonica and made a long note, then bending it as if playing the blues. "You try," he said, and he handed the instrument back to Tuan.

Tuan blew and tried to alter the tone, but he couldn't figure what to do with his mouth. More laughter erupted at the discordant result.

Tuan's friends Tim and Thieu, and Lay's friend Lin, also changed out of their school clothes, joined them on the porch.

"Your father's working in the rice paddies?" Hal asked Tuan.

"Yes, him work in rice," Tuan replied.

"Tomorrow we work in rice," added Tim.

"Hell, when I was your age I worked in the fields every day," Bo said.

"Yes, you same-same water buffalo," said Tim. He leaped away and shouted as Bo grabbed at him.

Tuan's father was the village chief. Tuan had told them his father had been in the army for many years, dating back to the war with the French. Even though he had fought as a Viet Minh against the French, he subsequently joined the South Vietnamese army, attaining the rank of Major. He had been wounded a few years before, and was now retired. Most of the men and older boys from the village were gone, off fighting, either as ARVN or Viet Cong. The few men left were not entirely free of the fighting. They occasionally wore the marginal uniforms of the RF-PF, the Regional Forces-Popular Forces, a form of local militia. The Americans called them "ruff-puffs," and had little confidence in their fighting abilities.

Bridge Ten

A female cat carrying a kitten trotted across the porch. Her fur was ragged, giving her a harried look. Her swollen teats swung from side to side with her efforts. Lay's little sisters ran after the cat, trying to get the kitten.

"You number ten," Tim was taunting Bo. "VC number one."

"VC number ten," said Bo. "We kill VC. You see dead VC."

"Arvin kill VC," Thieu reminded him.

"VC come, and we kill," Bo told the boys. "We cocky-dow," he said, drawing his finger across his neck.

Thieu and Tim hooted with laughter, trying to provoke a reaction from the strong, yet plodding American.

"I've got a good idea," Sonny told Hal. "I've been thinking about this for a while. We could all chip in and pay Lay's mother to cook a meal for us. We could have some authentic Vietnamese food, for a change."

"Hey, that's a great idea," Hal said. "I'll chip in."

"Ask your mother if she will cook for us," Sonny told Lay. "We pay her."

"You want she cook for you?" Lay asked.

"Yes, ask your mother," Sonny urged.

Lay explained the proposition to her mother, who listened, smiling. There was an exchange of words, and Lay asked Sonny, "How much you pay?"

"I don't know. How much she charge?"

This brought a longer discussion between Lay and her mother, and then Lay said, "She say, what you eat? She buy food in market. Maybe pig costs more than chicken. Or maybe you want fish?"

"I don't know. What do you guys want to eat?" Sonny asked.

"Let's try something simple for starters, like chicken," said Bo. "Some of their stuff looks pretty weird to me."

"Chicken sounds safe," agreed Hal.

43

"How about chicken?" Sonny asked Lay.

"Okay," Lay said, and conversation became more earnest as they entered into the heat of the negotiations.

"Seven hundred piaster," Lay finally told them.

"Seven hundred P!" Sonny declared. "Oh, mama-san, too much. That beaucoup!"

"No," Lay's mother replied. "Tee-tee."

"Seven hundred P? Damn," said Bo, "I can get a piece of ass for less than that!"

"Mama-san, three hundred piasters," Sonny said, perhaps a little too quickly.

Lay's mother acted insulted, clucking her tongue and looking at them with an indignant glare. They harangued back and forth, finally settling on five hundred piasters.

"Okay," Sonny agreed. "Maybe in two days?"

Lay's mother nodded, and the deal was set.

"Well, we'd better get back to the bridge," Sonny said. "Time to relieve Tennessee."

The three soldiers bowed to Lay's mother and thanked her for the hospitality. They were escorted to the highway by the kids.

Hal felt like a protector, towering over the frolicking children. They were here to defend the village from attacks and the terrors of war. Yet, he, too, felt protected when in the village; protected for a short measure of time from the Hill and all that was dirty and oppressive.

IV

"It's about time you guys showed up," Tennessee grumbled when Sonny, Hal and Bo got back to the bridge. A mask of dirt encircled his eyes, and the three laughed at his comical appearance.

"You look like a raccoon," Bo said.

"This bridge sucks!" Tennessee ranted.

"I'll take it," Sonny told him. "Go jump in the creek and cool off."

"I was about ready to do just that, whether anybody showed up or not."

Tennessee, carrying the two leaky air-mattresses, led Bo and Hal toward the creek, where they could hear the splashes and laughter of a few children that were already swimming. More kids joined the fray, and bedlam soon broke out in the little pool that was thick with leaping bodies. The smaller boys gathered around Bo, tugging on him and waiting to be thrown into the air, to land in the water with a great splash.

"I've got to get out of here. This place is driving me nuts," Tennessee told Hal.

"We've all got to get out of here, man," Hal replied. "We're one day closer to getting back to the World."

"No, I mean, I need to get away from this damn bridge."

"We could be on the Hill," Hal reminded him.

"Yeah, I know. It's just that sitting by this bridge all day and night is so stupid. Nobody wants this bridge. What the hell are we *doing*?"

"We're protecting the village. The guys on eleven don't have a village. Don't have shit. Anyways, nineteen more days and we'll be in Bangkok," said Hal.

"Nineteen days is a long time. One more day of this is too much."

The sun was edging toward the western horizon when the swimmers finally left the water. The children returned to the village for their dinners, while the soldiers went to the bunker to select meals from their stashes.

"Good old fucking C-rats," Tennessee grumbled, as he attacked a can of Beef Stew with his P-38 can-opener.

"Well, the mama-san is going to cook us a meal," said Sonny who, like the others, was hunkered over his heat-tab campfire tending his meal. "That'll be a nice change. If it's any good, maybe we can do it once a week."

"It sounds like she took you guys to the cleaners," Tennessee said. "Five hundred Ps. That's more than it would cost in a restaurant, probably."

"This'll be better than what you'd get in a restaurant. This is real Vietnamese food, man. Home cooking—not the shit you get in restaurants."

"You ever notice how everything in this place costs five bucks?" Tennessee asked. "I love it."

"It's just an experiment, man," Sonny said. "If it goes all right, I'll deal with the mama-san. I can talk her down some. We'll have a few more C-rats left over to sell to the gooks, too."

"Yeah, give them another chance to screw us," said Tennessee.

"Mellow out, dude," Sonny said, as he spooned food from his heated can. "Don't be so negative."

"You need some exercise," Hal told Tennessee, once they had finished their dinners. "Let's go for a walk to the village and back."

"Yeah, get his sour ass out of here," Sonny agreed.

"Okay," Tennessee acquiesced sullenly. "I'd like to see those dead gooks."

The sun was beginning to sink behind the mountains, and its yellow glare softened to mellower shades of red. With the cessation of traffic on the highway, the dust had settled and the air was purified.

As Hal and Tennessee neared the village they could see children gathered in the road—this, their evening playground. The sounds of their calls and laughter were almost musical. Birds, too, chirped and whisked among the branches in the trees' canopy, seeming to exalt in the sunset that was steadily growing to a deeper red.

A cluster of houses comprised the village. Most were made of stucco and painted in gay shades of yellow or blue. Others were made of clay or mud and had thatch roofs. Trees enclosed each house: banana trees; coconut trees; palm trees; trees bearing several varieties of fruit; and huge banyan trees, their arching branches forming a canopy. Front yards were barren plots demarcated by fences made of bamboo, thatch or barbed wire. In each spotless yard, grooves made parallel patterns where the ground had been swept. Adults sat on front porches and talked, while dogs sniffed and scratched at the dirt in their quest for leftovers.

The road's pavement yet radiated the day's heat, and groups of children ran barefoot over its surface. The boys and girls were, for the most part, grouped separately and engaged in varieties of play. A large troop of girls chanted to the rhythm of a swinging jump-rope. Two girls swung the rope, made of thick rubber-bands tied together, while several girls jumped in the middle. All the girls sang a song in time with the jumping. The boys, meanwhile, were playing a raucous game similar to kick the can. Standing in a line, the boys took turns throwing their sandals at a soda can set on the road. When someone hit the can there was a headlong rush for sandals, while whoever was "it" raced for the can. The game was complex and had different phases. Sometimes the contestants took turns throwing sandals at the can, like taking free-throws in basketball. The younger kids were playing games of tag, chasing one another around the periphery of the older children's contests. The village had taken on a surge of life that contrasted with the more subdued calm of day.

"Hey man," Tuan, standing with Thieu and Tim, greeted them. The three boys, too old to play the games of children, huddled conspiratorially beside the road. Each was gangly and delicate of feature, with fresh-cropped hair and clean white shirts. Tuan wore his Army baseball cap. "How, can I play?" he asked Hal, his perfect white teeth flashing into a smile.

"Okay, Tuan. You can play," Hal replied. He took the harmonica from his pocket and gave it to Tuan. As the boys walked with the soldiers, Tuan blew earnestly on the harmonica, experimenting with the notes it could produce.

"What are those signs?" Hal asked, pointing to the yellow sign that appeared over each yard entrance.

"Them name family," Tim explained.

They walked slowly down the street, away from the swarm of activity. Chickens scratched at the dirt alongside the road, eyeing and pecking the ground. An old man squatted in front of a little table, painting a piece of cloth. "What he do?" asked Hal.

"When he die, they put," Tim told him, waving his arms as he explained.

"They put on his grave when he dies?" Hal asked.

The boys nodded.

The old man smiled at them, exposing toothless gums. They watched him dab paint from small bowls and work carefully on the cloth. His eyes, surrounded by wrinkles, were fixed in concentration on his task. Chinese characters, exact and graceful, took shape on the canvas. There was something alien in the undertaking that struck Hal as the essence of Oriental fatalism, this careful preparation for death.

At the far end of the village was a board with pieces of paper affixed to it. Tuan explained that it was a local bulletin board with advertisements and area news. Hal felt like a tourist, the boys his guides, investigating an ancient, alien culture.

Beyond the far edge of the village, the bodies of the two NVA soldiers yet lay undisturbed. The day's heat had worked on the now bloated bodies, and the earlier pristine state of death had given way to the process of decay. The air was rank with the powerful odor of rotting flesh.

"Wow, what a mess!" Tennessee declared. After staring down at the forms for a moment, holding his hand over his nose, he said, "I've seen enough." They turned and started walking back.

"In America, are many cars, yes?" asked Tuan after they had walked a moment in silence.

"Oh, many cars," Hal said.

"You have?"

"When I get back, I buy car, yes."

Tuan nodded. "Yes, I think everybody rich in America."

"Not everybody. Some people poor," Hal said.

"We not rich," Tennessee said.

The boys laughed in disbelief. "In America everybody rich, I think," saidThieu.

"No, no, not everybody," Hal said.

"Yes," Tim said. "You have cars and tv and big house."

"What name Tuan in English?" Tuan asked.

"Oh, I don't know," Hal said, looking at Tennessee. "Tom?"

"Tom?" Tuan repeated, wearing a skeptical expression.

"Tommy," Tennessee said.

"Tommy!" Tuan cried with approval. "Number one! You call me, my name Tommy."

"What name me?" Tim asked eagerly.

"Tim American name," Hal told him.

Tim frowned. " Tim American name?"

"Timmy," Tennessee suggested.

"Timmy!" Tim repeated. "Timmy name me."

"My name? What name me?" Thieu asked.

"Thieu. That's a tough one," Hal said, thinking.

"Chuck?" Tennessee said.

Thieu couldn't pronounce the name, however, and they were forced to abandon it. After some deliberation, they finally settled on Billy.

"Billy! Number one!" Thieu cried in agreement.

As they walked back through the village the boys asked, "Name me!" Hal and Tennessee would respond with, "Billy," or "Tommy," or "Timmy." The boys repeated their names amid much laughter.

Hal and Tennessee left the boys at the edge of the village and continued toward the bridge. The road stretched before them as they walked, a straight line laid across the dimming flatlands and receding into obscurity.

When they got back to the bridge, Sonny and Bo were stretching the gates across the road. Hal and Tennessee checked the perimeter defenses, while the others prepared the bunker for nightfall. Once they had performed their evening duties, they were soon sitting on the bunker waiting for radio schedule. Each held a Bong Son bomber and was ticking another day off his personal calendar.

"Those dead gooks are gross," Tennessee said.

"They're getting pretty bad," Hal agreed.

"I'd like to know what the story is," Sonny said. "They're shooting NVA only a mile from our position, and we don't know shit."

"A pacified area! What a crock of shit," Hal said.

"No shit," Sonny agreed. "This area has always been a VC stronghold, even when they were fighting the French. The First Cav got their *asses* kicked here in sixty-six."

"It makes you wonder who's VC," said Tennessee.

"You never know what they're thinking," Bo said.

"Yeah, it's like they're smiling and saying 'fuck you' at the same time," Hal said.

"You might be surprised who's VC around here," Sonny said.

They listened to the radio schedule, performed as if by rote. Sonny turned the radio off and they sat quietly in the near-darkness.

"I've got the plan!" Tennessee told Hal suddenly. "We'll hitch a ride to Quin Nhon."

"What? What are you talking about?" Hal asked.

"Yeah man, it's perfect. We can make it there and back in a day, easy."

"Are you nuts?" Hal said. "Hitch-hike to Quin Nhon? What if we get caught?"

"Who's gonna catch us? Martin won't be down here. They're too busy working on the perimeter up there. He wouldn't miss a minute of that project. The timing is perfect."

"There's plenty of lifers on the road," Hal said.

"We just look like we know what we're doing," Tennessee said. "We'll be all right."

"You dudes are crazy!" Sonny said." You're just going to hitch a ride to Quin Nhon?"

"We just need you to cover for us," Tennessee said.

"What if Martin *does* come down here?"

"You just say we're in the village having a soda. If he doesn't go for it, it's our ass, not yours."

"Man, we have R&R coming up in just two weeks," Hal said.

"If I have to spend another day on this damn bridge, I'll go nuts," Tennessee said. "Come on man, we can get laid and smoke some opium. It'll be great!"

"Unless we get caught."

"What are they going to do to us? Send us to Nam? It don't mean nothing, man."

Hal considered the proposition. The thought of getting away from the bridge for a day, to be out on the road instead of sitting in its dust, was indeed attractive. Tennessee was right, it didn't mean nothing.

"You guys cover for us, and tomorrow night we'll pull your watches," Tennessee said.

"You're on," Bo said, responding to the possibility of an uninterrupted night's sleep.

Sonny's laugh boomed. "Man, you two dudes are too much! Gonna hitch-hike to Quin Nhon!"

"It *would* be nice to get out of here for a day," Hal said. "This bridge is definitely getting old."

"Yeah man, that's the spirit," Tennessee said. "It'll be great!"

Darkness grew around them while they talked, and the buzz and croaks of the night's creatures rose as background to their conversation.

"Time to call it a day," Sonny finally declared.

"One day less in this man's Army," Tennessee said. "Tomorrow Quin Nhon, man."

The bunker became quiet after Sonny, Tennessee and Bo left Hal alone to his watch. Hal let his hearing adjust to the chorus of nocturnal sounds, much like waiting for night vision, and contemplated what Tennessee was getting him into. But in the final analysis, Tennessee was absolutely right. *It don't mean nothing.*

V

"We just wait for the right ride," Tennessee was saying the next morning as they sat on the bunker drinking coffee.

A motorcycle carrying a man with two pigs puttered past, headed toward Quin Nhon. Each pig was in its individual reed basket and lashed to the side of the machine.

"And the return trip?" Hal asked.

"No sweat. With all the traffic on this road? We'll have our pick of rides."

"Yeah, okay," Hal said. Despite his misgivings, he was getting excited at the prospect of the trip. There was something attractive, too, about taking a risk.

"As long as you dudes are going, you could get me some liquid O," Sonny said. "Here's a carton of cigarettes—that should be enough."

"Hey, and get me some Obesitol," said Bo.

Hal and Tennessee looked at each other. "Yeah, sure," Tennessee replied.

"Oh man, what you want to get *that* shit for?" Sonny asked.

Obesitol was a French diet drug marketed in bottles containing a sweetish liquid. Chug a bottle, and you were up all night. The last time Bo drank Obesitol he had spent his entire watch with his M-16 locked and loaded, pointed at the ground where he claimed to hear VC tunneling beneath him. Nobody had slept much that night.

"I just like it," Bo said with the stubborn look he got when his mind was set. He handed Tennessee a carton of cigarettes.

"Oh, man," said Sonny, shaking his head.

Tennessee found an empty sandbag to carry the cigarettes, and they waited, growing impatient as buses and lambrettas passed before them.

"It's going to be a hot one," Sonny said, mopping at his forehead with his "drive-on rag," a green towel that he kept draped over his shoulder.

"I don't aim to be here to find out," Tennessee said.

Finally, an Army deuce-and-a-half approached. Tennessee and Hal stood up and stepped toward the road, watching the truck closely in order to discern the cab's interior.

When the truck drew nearer, they could see the two occupants. Both wore sunglasses, and the driver was smoking a joint.

Tennessee waved his arms, and it stopped next to them. "We're trying to get to Quin Nhon," he told the driver.

"We're going there, man. Hop in the back," the driver said. Hal noted that the sergeant sitting beside the driver was also holding a joint.

"All right!" Tennessee shouted, and he gathered the bag of cigarettes.

"Hey man," Sonny whispered to Hal, "don't get any Obesitol for Bo."

"Don't worry," Hal replied. "We'll tell him we couldn't find any."

Hal and Tennessee climbed into the back of the truck where five other soldiers were seated. The truck started moving, changing gears and thumping over the bridge. One of the soldiers handed Hal a joint.

"Where are you guys headed?" Hal asked him.

"Cam Rahn Bay. We're going on R and R," he replied, shouting over the engine noise.

The truck sped down the highway, and the wind that swept across the open back of the truck felt cool and refreshing. As they drove past Bridge Eleven, Hal and Tennessee yelled and waved at Cathcart, Bradford and Day, who were sitting on their bunker drinking coffee. The three looked up, and Cathcart's jaw dropped when he made eye contact with Hal. He raised an arm to point and was shouting something to the others. Tennessee howled like a wolf, and the truck was past, a cloud of dust covering their wake.

The Hill loomed above them as the truck labored over Bong Son Pass. Tennessee was pointing to the Hill and shouting something to the two soldiers next to him. The three laughed into the wind that swept over them, tousling their hair. The scrubby vegetation of the roadside gave way to barren dirt near the top of the Hill. Hal could make out shirtless figures toiling amidst the perimeter's snarl of concertina wire. They were working, he knew, under the watchful eyes of Sergeant Martin and Lieutenant Edmonds.

The highway descended the south side of the pass, and they were back in the flats, rice paddies spreading around them. Rocky tree-covered mounds stood as islands amid the otherwise perfectly flat valley floor. The hills rose in sheer cliffs, a scattering of rock that broke the symmetry of the paddies, as though seedling mountains had taken hold. They passed farm houses, where chickens and pigs darted from their path, and roared through villages, the driver honking the horn and swerving around pedestrians that appeared unconcerned with their passing. They overtook slower vehicles—lambrettas and groaning buses--sometimes jumping back into the right lane to avoid oncoming trucks. Trees cut their view, giving them a moment of shade, before dispersing and delivering them back into the glare of the sun. The dark blue of the sky was in sharp contrast to the green of the land, lending objects an individual intensity, so sharp and beautiful it almost hurt Hal's eyes.

Alongside the road harvested rice was spread to dry on grass mats. Children wielding sticks and palm-leaf switches vigilantly guarded the rice from chickens. Women trotted beneath their yokes, faces hidden by their conical straw hats. Bicycles wobbled in and out of the road, deaf to the truck's blaring horn.

The truck geared down when they began to encounter heavy traffic. They were approaching Phu Cat, a town made prominent by the neighboring US military base. The city center was a beehive of activity. The road narrowed, and the truck crawled through an undisciplined snarl of vehicles and pedestrians. Diesel smoke hung like a mist in the air. People filled the street-fronts, entering and exiting shops, haggling with produce vendors, crowding around food stalls where smoke rose from charcoal fires, or moving against the throng with a purposeful, frantic energy. The streets were hot and heavy with the smell of fish. Litter abounded in the street--plastic, paper and discarded produce--the by-products of commerce. Concrete gutters with boards laid across as bridges ran in front of the line of shops. A little boy squatted in the gutter with his pants pulled down.

"Check it out!" cried one of the soldiers. "Taking a shit right on Main Street! They're fucking animals, man!"

They passed a Vietnamese truck with soldiers jammed in the back. When they saw the Americans, the ARVN soldiers waved. The soldier next to Hal started yelling, "Fuck you! You chicken-shits!" He turned to Hal with a savage expression. "Those chicken-shits ran out on us, man," he said. "Left our asses hanging while they ran for their dear lives. We lost Mason and Bradford because of it."

"Fuck it, man," one of the others told him, as the Vietnamese truck disappeared into the maze of traffic. "It don't mean nothing."

"Yeah, forget that shit," the soldier sitting next to Tennessee added. "We're going on R and R."

"Where you going?" Tennessee asked.

"Bangkok."

"Hey, we are, too! In eighteen more days," Tennessee said.

"When you get there, you've got to go to the fish gardens," the soldier told Tennessee. "It's these gardens with ponds, and with benches under the trees along the shores. You can rent a fishing pole and catch fish. Anyways, ask for the mama-san, and tell her you want to smoke the pipe. They have this little gazebo sort of hidden by hedges. They have this big water-pipe, and you can sit in there and watch people fishing while smoking some dynamite pot."

"Hey, that sounds cool," Tennessee said enthusiastically. "We'll have to try that," he shouted to Hal.

Once they were free of the city traffic they were barreling through the countryside again. They passed joints back and forth and shouted over the rushing wind. "So that's what you guys do? You guard that bridge?"

"That's it," Hal replied.

"That looks like good duty!"

"It sucks," said Tennessee.

"It beats humping it and getting your ass shot up all the time."

"Have a beer," a soldier said, as he pulled bottles of Thai beer from his pack and passed them around.

The truck slowed again as they neared An Nhon, another sizable city. Diesel fumes grew thick and vied with the smells of fish and rotting garbage. A squalor of shanties, built of wooden pallets, corrugated tin, cardboard and plastic, lined road. The structures were the product of urban growth forced by the fighting and destruction in the countryside.

The soldier sitting next to Hal took a final swallow of beer, turned, and flung the empty bottle at a woman pedestrian. Hal watched the bottle sail through the air and make a direct hit, full in the woman's face. As she went down to her knees the soldier cheered, "Bull's eye!"

Hal wheeled around, yelling, "What the hell was *that* for?"

The soldier, laughing and pointing at the growing knot of people behind them, snarled angrily, "Hey, it's just a gook, man."

"Yeah, mellow out dude," one of the other soldiers told him.

"But she's an innocent civilian," Hal said.

"She's probably VC."

Hal looked back. A girl was crying and a crowd was gathering around the fallen woman. The witnesses were pointing up the street to their truck and speaking with animated gestures. Hal watched with horror and impotent fury until the scene was obscured by the heavy traffic. He turned back to his fellow occupants, who were passing a joint, like nothing had happened. He caught Tennessee's eye and they traded a brief awkward look before Tennessee lowered his eyes and turned away quickly.

They broke free of the city and picked up speed again, passing relocation camps—rows of identical white buildings enclosed by concertina wire. The Vietnamization process of securing the countryside necessitated relocating whole villages from vast rural areas and transporting them to these depressing compounds, where the occupants, subsisting in idle desperation, awaited permission to return to their ancestral homes.

Finally, they were nearing Quin Nhon, a large city and military center. On one side of the highway was a sprawling dump, comprising acres of moldering trash and garbage. Children and old ladies were sifting through the mounds of filth for anything of value. An Army dump truck full of trash was moving through the mounds. Boys were racing after the truck, leaping at it, and climbing onto the back of the moving vehicle. They rummaged frantically through the truck's contents, throwing valuables off to the boys running alongside.

"Let us off before we get downtown," Tennessee yelled up front to the driver. "I don't think we want to be downtown," he told Hal. "That's where the MPs will be."

The character of the road was changing rapidly as they proceeded into the increasing congestion. Dwellings condensed into a solid growth of shanties, each demarcated by a tiny barren plot of soil. Shops and restaurants began to displace the residential areas, and ahead they could see the taller hotels of downtown.

The truck stopped at a shouted command from Tennessee. After a quick look up and down the street, Tennessee and Hal jumped down, waved to the driver, and hurried off the main road and up a side-street.

Store-fronts crowded the sidewalks along the narrow avenue. The throng of shoppers overflowed the walkways into the street, where handcarts filled with goods moved stealthily through the crowd. Vendors selling food along the curbs raised a strong mix of odors that permeated the air. Hal and Tennessee walked a block and watched their back-trail to be sure they hadn't been spotted. They were the only Americans to be seen on the street, and towering over the rest of the populace, they seemed to be advertising their presence.

"We are definitely nuts," said Hal, noting the curious looks they inspired from the Vietnamese as they passed.

"So far, so good, man," Tennessee replied. "Hey, this place is far out!"

Across the street was a cafe that bustled with an early lunch hour crowd. "Let's get something to eat," Hal suggested, eager to get off the street.

"Good idea. I'm starving," Tennessee agreed.

From their table they had a good view of the approach from the main road and of the tireless activity of commerce on the street. Behind the counter a woman stood over a steaming fire shaking pots. Girls carried platters of food to the tables, trailing the aroma of spices.

One of the girls approached their table and asked something, presumably requesting their order, in rapid Vietnamese.

"We want lunch," Tennessee told her.

"I don't think she speaks much English," said Hal. He pointed at the noodle dish on the next table and said, "Same-same for me. And one coca-cola."

The girl responded in Vietnamese, but Hal could only make out the word "coca-cola."

"Same-same me," Tennessee told her, holding up two fingers.

The girl nodded and retreated to the back, giggling.

A man approached them from the street. "Hello GI," he said, smiling and looking around furtively. "You want buy watch?" he asked, and he raised his sleeve to reveal several watches attached to his arm.

"No papa-san," Tennessee said. "We no want. We have," and he held up his arm to show that he was wearing a watch.

The man inspected Tennessee's watch and shook his head sadly. "I have number one watch," the man said, raising his sleeve again, eager to display his line of superior watches. Gold teeth gleamed when he smiled.

"No, no, papa-san. We no want," Tennessee said firmly.

The man frowned, incredulous, but he continued to hover over their table, alternately smiling and glancing to the street. He talked to the man at the next table and sat down across from him. The two laughed over something the man said, and they both sat watching the Americans.

The girl returned with their food. Shrimp, fish and vegetables were mixed with noodles, and they found the spicy dish to be delicious. "Now this is the life," said Tennessee, taking a sip of coke.

Hal nodded vigorously, smiling around a mouthful of noodles. "This beats the bridge any day, man," he said. "This is like another world." Forgotten was the list of various charges they would be eligible for if they were caught.

"Man, check it out," Tennessee said, nodding toward two girls walking on the sidewalk across from the restaurant. They wore identical sky-blue ao dais, the long, supple material caressing the ground as they walked. Their black hair, combed long down their backs, gleamed like silk. They held their conical hats at an angle, almost as instruments of expression, half concealing their faces.

"Wow, unbelievable," Hal sighed. The purity of their beauty was stunning.

Boys began to gather around their table. "You buy?" one of them asked, and he displayed an array of lighters. Another boy produced a collection of peace-symbol medallions. "Number one! You buy!"

"No, no," Hal replied. "We no buy." The watch man, when Hal happened to look at him, smiled and started to pull his sleeve up again.

"You want boom-boom?" asked one of the boys.

"Yes, we want boom-boom," Tennessee confirmed. "We want number one boom-boom."

"Yes, number one boom-boom," said the boy. "Five dollar."

"Okay. Where we go? How far?" Tennessee asked.

"Not far," said the boy, moving closer and speaking confidentially.

"No MPs?"

"No, no MPs come," assured the boy.

"We want camsaht," Hal said. "You can get for us?"

"Yes, we go," the boy said eagerly. "I get for you."

They paid for the meal and followed the boy up the street.

A man wearing sunglasses emerged from a doorway. "You change money?" he asked. He displayed a wad of Vietnamese bills as he looked furtively up and down the street.

"You change? How much?" Tennessee asked.

"Oh, number one, number one. How much you have?"

Tennessee pulled money from his pocket and counted it under the intense scrutiny of the Vietnamese. The US military, in an attempt to foil black marketing activities, paid soldiers with mpcs, "military payment certificates." This succeeded in greatly reducing US currency in the economy, but rampant inflation constantly reduced the value of Vietnamese currency relative to the US dollar. Since the value of the mpc was greater than the official exchange rate, Vietnamese entrepreneurs were able to reap considerable profits from illicit currency transactions.

The man accepted the mpcs, deftly counted the exchange in dongs, and handed Tennessee the money. Smiling, he receded into the doorway's shadows

The boy led them onto a smaller street, and they turned again. They were out of the commercial district, and the streets were considerably less crowded. Children gawked at them from doorways as they passed decrepit tenements, and dogs barked at them from littered alleys.

"I thought it wasn't far," Tennessee said.

"Not far. No MP come here," the boy assured them.

They turned onto another street, and ahead they could see two girls standing beside an open doorway. The Rolling Stones blared "Satisfaction" from a tape-deck somewhere inside the door. The girls smiled when they saw the Americans approach. One had several gold teeth, and the other bore tattoos on her arm and on the back of one hand.

"We ought to be able to do better than this," Hal said.

"Let's at least get a beer. The boy-san can run and get our pot."

"My name Crystal," the girl with the tattoos told Hal, taking his arm and pulling him toward the door.

"Me Suzi," the other girl said as she grasped Tennessee. "You come inside."

They entered a dimly lit room furnished with two tables and several chairs. Two American soldiers were sitting at one of the tables drinking beer, each sporting a girl on his lap. The occupants regarded the newcomers briefly before resuming their banter.

The girls seated Hal and Tennessee at the open table and went to get beer from the mama-san, who was sitting behind a counter that displayed liquor and cigarettes.

Hal paid the boy for the pot and watched him dart out the door. The girls brought their beers and Hal took a long drink. "That hits the spot," he shouted to Tennessee above the blare of music.

The other two Americans drifted into the back rooms with their escorts after negotiating with the mama-san.

Suzi and Crystal slid into their laps, and Tennessee bought them cokes. The mama-san brought the drinks and accepted their money. "Number one girls," she said.

"We go make movie," Crystal told Hal, motioning to the back rooms. Her practiced, eager fingers fluttered over his body. Hal looked at her tattoos— names scrawled on her arm in crude blue ink and a small cross on the back of her hand.

The boy returned with plastic bags of rolled joints. Tennessee ordered a coke for the boy from the mama-san. Hal lit a joint and passed it to Tennessee and then lit another for himself. They sat smoking and sipping beer, while the girls bounced on their laps.

"Five dollar," Crystal told Hal. "I love you long time."

"You souvenir me."

"Souvenir! Oh, no souvenir," she said. "Sin loi, min-yoi. No money no honey." She feigned outrage, but her fingers redoubled their efforts.

The two soldiers came out of the back rooms and left. The mama-san advanced on their table again, having grown impatient at their delay. "Five dollar! Tee-tee for number one girl."

Crystal's hand had found its way inside Hal's pants, and his desire became an immediate and imperative command. His hand moved inside her shirt, and he massaged her small, firm breasts. "I think I'm going to go for it," he finally told Tennessee.

"Me too," Tennessee said, reaching into his pocket for money.

They each paid the mama-san five dollars. Her eyes gleamed when she saw the American dollars, and her wrinkled hands eagerly closed around them.

Hal and Tennessee followed the girls to a back hallway with doors to four bedrooms. Hal and Crystal went into one of the bedrooms, a cubicle barely large enough for the bed. A curtain was drawn across the window, obscuring the room in shadow. They clutched at each other. Hal struggled to work the girl's shirt off, while her more practiced fingers efficiently undid his pants.

"I be right back," Crystal said.

Hal watched her dash from the room and return with a pan of water. She washed his penis, sliding it in her hands, inspecting it and watching it swell.

They moved to the bed. Naked in the dim light, she looked dumpy. The breasts that had felt like perfect melons were adolescent protuberances hanging over the swell of her belly. Her pubic hairs were scanty and wispy, converging into a little duck-tail, like a baby Elvis. She grasped his penis and guided it inside her. The tidal aroma of sex rose with his urgent thrustings. Hal's urgent release was almost immediate.

Hal lay on the bed, his head propped up on a pillow, as Crystal left to wash herself. He could hear Tennessee's shrill laughter from the next room. A picture of Pam, dressed for the prom, flickered in his mind. He quickly dismissed the thought and lit a joint. He heard voices in the hallway and the rapid footfalls of somebody running.

The door burst open and Crystal rushed in. "You go! MP come! MP!" she cried.

Hal lunged to his feet. "MP?"

"Yes! You go!" she said, and they frantically gathered up Hal's clothes.

Hal snubbed out the joint and threw it under the bed. He pulled his pants on and started working into his boots, hopping and staggering toward the window. Crystal had drawn the curtain back and was urging him. "Hurry!" she whispered.

Hal hiked one leg over the sill and slid out the window. Tennessee was coming out of the neighboring window head-first, and he tumbled onto the ground. Crystal handed Hal his shirt through the window. "Hurry!" she said, pointing to the narrow alley.

Hal and Tennessee wrestled with their shirts as they rushed up the alley, their boot-laces trailing behind them. An old man sharpening a knife looked up, startled, as they ran by him. They turned up another alley and followed it to where it crossed the street.

"Damn, that was close," Tennessee gasped. They stood panting and looking around for any pursuit. They noted only a few Vietnamese on the street, so after lacing their boots, they darted across to the other side.

"Hey, what the hell?" said Tennessee, who was looking down the main street.

A block away was the whore house from which they had run. Three American soldiers were standing outside the door, but they weren't MPs. Two girls were talking to them. "Oh man," Hal said when he saw Crystal come out of the door and take hold of a soldier's arm. Collectively, the girls coaxed the Americans inside.

"We got hustled!" Tennessee exclaimed.

"Oh *man*," Hal said, starting to laugh. "I guess they needed a quick turnover."

"Yeah, they're sly, all right."

"You looked good coming through that window."

"She got me moving, all right," Tennessee said, laughing now, too.

"That's the fastest I've ever seen you move."

"You were moving right out yourself," Tennessee said. "I guess we got our money's worth, anyways."

"Yeah, I guess," Hal said. "Now where the hell are we?" he asked.

They set off up the street and away from the whore house. Soon they were wandering aimlessly through the maze of narrow lanes.

"Hey man, where you go?" A boy wearing an Army fatigue cap was following them. "You want boom-boom?"

"No boom-boom," said Tennessee. "We want opium. You can find?"

"Ofium? Yes, I know where," the boy replied, nodding his head emphatically. "You come."

They followed their new guide, no longer caring where they were. The boy led them to a house on another street. He talked in rapid Vietnamese to the woman who came to the door. A little boy and girl clutched at the lady's leg. Tennessee showed her the cartons of cigarettes he was carrying in his sandbag. She smiled and motioned them into the house.

Hal could smell the sweet aroma of opium drifting from the back rooms of the house. He smiled at the children and they stared back mutely. The woman directed them to another room, where a man lay on a wide wooden platform. There were grass mats spread on the platform, and the man's head rested on a pillow. He smiled at them through glazed eyes. An opium pipe and various paraphernalia were on the mat beside him, and here the opium smell was much stronger.

Tennessee gave the woman the cigarettes, and they took turns lying on the mat beside the man. Hal watched the man roll the opium into a black tar-ball, heat it, and work the pliant mass onto the bowl of the pipe, probing it with a tool that looked like a nut-pick. The opium bubbled and sizzled as Hal drew on the pipe in a slow, deep inhalation. The nut-pick deftly herded the burning ooze to the hole, so that it all went up the pipe in the form of a smooth, sweet smoke. Hal held the smoke in, the man smiling at him, then exhaled a huge cloud. A wave of euphoria washed over his body. "Man, this stuff is great!" he said and laughed. His voice sounded like it was coming from the next room.

The children drifted in and out of the room, pausing to watch the Americans. The woman brought Hal a cold coke while Tennessee took his turn at the pipe. Two cartons of cigarettes bought them twelve bowls of opium apiece, plus the half-time cokes.

"Hooo-ee!" said Tennessee, getting up slowly from the mat. He glided in slow motion toward Hal. "That's some good shit, man."

"Man, I'm high as a kite," Hal said. His jaws felt numb as he spoke. They laughed, and the man laughed too, apparently pleased with his work.

Tennessee looked at his watch. It was mid-afternoon. "Right on schedule," he said. Finding this fact funny, he broke into giggles.

"We're on one hell of a schedule," Hal said, and their laughter intensified.

Tennessee gave the remaining cigarettes to the woman for the bottle of liquid opium Sonny had ordered. The boy materialized, and they followed him back onto the street for the trip back to the highway.

The pace of life on the streets had slowed in the afternoon heat. The shops had become refuges from the sun, where merchants sat with friends and customers, sipping iced tea and watching the torpid stirrings under the outside glare.

Hal and Tennessee trailed behind the boy, advancing like gods past the ranks of stores, nodding and waving to the occupants. The heat was intense on the street, and they were soon dripping with sweat.

"Hey, papa-san," Tennessee yelled, flashing the peace-sign at an old man towing a cartload of bananas. The man smiled and made an uncertain peace-sign in reply. Hal and Tennessee laughed uproariously. The din from the main street increased as they drew nearer. The highway was angry with dust, and the unceasing chaos of traffic a stark contrast to the quietude just inland. As they approached the highway their sense of caution returned, though at a much reduced level.

Tennessee put some coins into the boy's hand, and they crossed the highway. Tennessee darted in front of an Army truck, waving his arms. "Hey, where are you going?" he yelled.

The driver geared down and shouted, "Phu Cat. Hop in."

"All right!" Tennessee cried, and they ran to the rear of the truck.

Hal felt like he was wrapped in velvet as he rolled up onto the bed of the truck.

The truck ran through its scale of gears, and they were again weaving through the street's congestion. There were no other passengers in the back, and they stood behind the cab, looking over the top.

"This is cool, man," Tennessee shouted. Their sense of acceptance, and of abandonment, was complete.

The truck retraced their route up Highway One, past stores, coke stands, bars; past dunes of trash; past miles of barbed concertina wire stretched like giant slinky toys. They entered An Nhon and passed the spot where the woman had been struck down. The street looked innocent now, but Hal felt a stab of guilt.

They broke free of the city and were grateful to be moving again and to feel the wind on their faces. Hal thrust his face into the wind, like a dog in the back of a pick-up. The countryside passed in a series of tableaus, like they were watching a movie: A farmer in the field, standing with his hand resting on a water buffalo beside him, both pausing to look up at the highway; A mange-ridden dog sitting next to the road, his pale, pinkish skin looking like a pig's hide, his head bowed as though contemplating death; Three country women squatting near the road, their yokes propped on the ground, spitting into the dirt and exposing their beetle-blackened horse teeth in laughter.

The truck's pace slowed again when they reached Phu Cat, and they were once again subjected to the full power of the sun. The truck stopped and they disembarked. "Thanks, man," Tennessee shouted to the driver.

"Good luck," the driver replied, and he pulled back onto the road and faded into the dusty traffic.

Tennessee laughed. "You are a bust, man. You should see your eyes."

Hal glanced at Tennessee. He looked derelict in his faded, dusty uniform, the sweaty bandana tied around his neck and his red hound-dog eyes. "You should talk. Your eyes are like neon lights."

They were standing in the center of the city, near the market, where a stream of straw sun hats bobbed and flowed around the ranks of stalls.

Lambrettas and motorcycles weaved up and down the street, but they could see no military vehicles.

"Let's check out the market," Hal suggested.

Tennessee looked at his watch. "Okay, we have plenty of time."

They walked toward the hub of industry, where shops stretched in lines like carnival booths. Tin and tarps formed a patchwork of roofing that provided shade for the merchants and shoppers. The mixed garble of barter rose in volume as they neared the complex. An old lady was arguing with one of the merchants, her voice rising into a shriek. She held a taro root and waved it as she spilled forth her invective, her conical sun hat bobbing up and down. The other lady matched her attack, pointing at the taro root and unleashing a stream of words, a look of insult animating her face. Only the laughter of the spectators indicated that this wasn't some mortal contest.

Hal and Tennessee walked slowly down the aisle, watching the frantic, insistent commerce. In contrast to the mute rows of goods in the American supermarket, here the competing wares had spokesmen acclaiming the merits and superiority of their products. They walked past booths with sweet potatoes, cinnamon, cassava, and peanuts. There were booths with mangoes, bananas, papaya, and durian. American black market goods were in abundance: cigarettes; whiskey; beer; military apparel; radios. Women called to them as they passed, holding up strange vegetables.

"Let's get some bananas," Tennessee said.

A lady held up a bunch of bananas and said something to them in Vietnamese.

"Mama-san," Tennessee said, pointing at the bananas. "How much we pay?"

The lady smiled and nodded, apparently unable to understand English.

"Mama-san," Tennessee tried again. "How much we pay?" He took some money out of his pocket and showed it to her.

The lady pointed at Tennessee's money, indicating how much she wanted.

"Oh mama-san," Tennessee said. "Beaucoup! Beaucoup!"

The lady reacted as though insulted, clucking like an enraged hen. She said something in Vietnamese, and the ladies in the neighboring booths laughed. They were surrounded now by the upturned straw hats, and Hal felt trapped. The ladies' eyes crinkled as they exchanged witticisms, each received with raucous laughter.

"Mama-san, I pay you for bananas," Tennessee said as he held out his hand.

The lady rolled her eyes and said something that was greeted with howls of laughter from the assemblage of women.

"She's messing with you, man," Hal said.

"Yeah, she's fucking with my head," Tennessee agreed. "I don't know what's going on."

The woman finally selected the desired coins from Tennessee's hand, and the two Americans extracted themselves, bowing and smiling at the laughing Vietnamese.

Hal took a banana and peeled it. "These are good," He said. The short, plump bananas were sweeter and of a richer texture than the bananas found in US supermarkets.

"They're good, but I probably paid three times the going price, though."

"It was worth it to get out of there."

They resumed their walk through the market, taking in the strange sights and smells. Women sold live chickens that were arrayed patiently on the ground with legs bound. A lady squatting on a curb, sold tiny sparrow-like birds amassed in round reed baskets that looked like large bee-hives. Each basket was alive with swarming, fluttering wings. The lady alternately put each basket in a shallow puddle, and the water exploded as frantic feathers sought the cooling bath.

They walked the final row of booths and emerged back into the sunlight. On the highway there were yet no American vehicles in sight. "Let's walk and get out of downtown," said Tennessee. "I don't like standing here."

"Yeah, we don't want to get caught now," Hal agreed.

After the bustle of the market, the sidewalk seemed quiet. They passed clothing stores and tire shops while looking back down the highway for a ride. A woman breast-feeding her baby hastily covered her breast when she saw them. Beside her was a meat counter where flies spun in lazy circles.

They walked uncounted blocks before the nature of the city began to change, and the crowded stores were finally left behind. Their vigil for a ride was like a nervous tic, their heads darting back at the first sound of on-coming traffic behind them. Yet no American vehicles materialized.

"Fuck this," Tennessee said when they approached a coke stand, "let's get a coke."

They sat at a table and ordered cokes from one of the girls. The establishment was a larger version of Lay's stand. When the drinks arrived, Hal held his cold glass against his forehead.

"It's good to be off the street," Hal said. "We can sit here and watch for our ride."

"You beaucoup hot," said the girl, giggling at their sweaty, bedraggled appearance.

"Beaucoup hot," Hal agreed.

"Where you go?" she asked, eager to practice her English.

"Bong Son," said Hal.

"Ah, Bong Son," she said, and she interpreted the information to the other girls. "Ah, Bong Son," they all agreed.

Boys moved in like a flock of vultures, asking, "You want boom-boom?"

"We no want boom-boom."

"You want camsaht?"

"No want camsaht."

"You change money."

"No change money."

"You buy," said one, holding a board with key-rings and roach-clips.

"No, no! Dee-dee!" Tennessee shouted and waved his arms. "Man, these kids are driving me nuts."

The boys moved off a few steps, to form a sullen pack. "GI number ten," said one.

"Where the hell is our ride?" asked Tennessee, looking down the road.

"It had better hurry up," Hal said. Soon it would be too late for anybody traveling as far as Bong Son. "I don't know which would be worse—to get busted, or to have to spend the night around here somewhere." Hal was beginning to wish they had brought their M 16s, equipment they were supposed to have in their possession at all times according to military regulations. But they had decided to leave the rifles behind so they wouldn't have to worry about losing them.

"Don't even *talk* about spending the night out," said Tennessee. "Shit!"

"You buy, okay," said one of the boys, holding up a watch. The boys were moving in again, like predators sensing an injured animal.

"We'll probably get a case of the clap, to boot," said Hal.

"So you get a shot of penicillin in the ass and drive on," Tennessee said. In fact, gonorrhea was more prevalent among the GIs than the common cold. The most famous case was Mimms, who had gone on R and R to Hawaii to meet his wife and had passed on a dose of clap to her that he'd unwittingly contracted.

"Me shine shoes," one of the boys said, and they laughed at the Americans' scruffy boots.

"Oh man, dee-dee!" Tennessee said more forcefully.

"Hey, what's that?" Hal asked, pointing down the highway. A truck with a huge crane was coming out of the city.

"Army Engineers," Tennessee said. They jumped up and watched the truck advance. The boys began cheering and shouting, like a gallery of hecklers. Tennessee ran into the street waving his arms. "Where you going, man," he asked when the truck pulled up beside him.

"English," said the soldier sitting next to the driver. "Hop on the back. Have a hit," he added, offering them a Bomber.

They puffed on the joint and then climbed onto the bed of the truck. The boys were yelling and jumping up and down as they pulled away, and Hal and Tennessee waved at them.

A couple of the boys flipped them the finger. "Those little shit-heads," Tennessee yelled, flipping them back. He laughed at the increased frenzy his gesture induced.

"Ah, the hell with them. We're home free, man," said Hal.

"Yeah!" Tennessee cried, and they slapped hands. "I'll smoke to that," Tennessee added, and he took two joints from his pocket.

"Let's get up there," Hal said, pointing up to the crane. They climbed the lattice-work of steel, to sit high above the earth on the heaving shaft.

"Hey, now this is living!" Tennessee shouted, cupping the joint to his chest, away from the wind.

Hal felt like he was floating through the countryside, as though he had left his body and was a hawk soaring high in the wind. He laughed at the reactions of the Vietnamese. The adults looked up at them with curious, uncertain smiles, but the children, as though in league with their depravity, reacted with animation, shouting, jumping and running after them. From his vantage point, Hal could see far out into the rice paddies, where farmers walked along the dikes, bent for home after the day's labors.

The euphoria dissipated when the Hill came into sight. It arose like a memory of all they had escaped, for however briefly. The specter of the dirt compound on top loomed like a concentration camp. The truck labored over the pass, and the Bong Son valley opened below them.

"Home sweet home," Hal said, as the truck coasted downhill into the familiar flatlands.

"We escaped for a day, man. They can't take that away from us," Tennessee said.

They approached Bridge Eleven, and Hal could see Cathcart, Day, Reep, and Bradford sitting on their bunker. They looked destitute, hunkered amongst the sandbags.

"Yoo-hoo! Boys!" Tennessee shouted. He laughed when all four rose to their feet in surprise.

"Quin Nhon is lovely this time of year!" Hal shouted to them. He could hear them calling and hooting. "You crazy fuckers!" Cathcart shouted, as they raced past.

They sped down the straight stretch of road to Bridge Ten. Sonny and Bo were sitting on the bunker. "Damn, I was starting to get worried," said Sonny, when they pulled to a stop.

Hal and Tennessee jumped down from the truck. "Thanks, man," they called to the driver, and the truck rolled back onto the highway, continuing north to LZ English.

"No sign of Martin?" asked Hal.

"Nope," Sonny replied. "No lifers come. You guys lucked out."

"We pulled it off," Tennessee said. "What did I tell you, man?" he asked Hal.

"Did you guys get my liquid O?" asked Sonny.

"Right here," Tennessee said, and he pulled the bottle from his pocket.

"How about my Obesitol?" asked Bo.

"We couldn't find any," Tennessee said.

"What? A drug store should have had some," Bo said, frowning.

"We tried a couple of places," Hal said, "but we couldn't find any."

"You don't need that shit anyway," Sonny said. "Try some of this instead and mellow out." He was dabbing some of the black opium onto Bombers.

Bo accepted a joint, but he looked at Hal and Tennessee with a skeptical expression.

They smoked joints while heating their C-rations, enjoying the quiet of the fading day.

Hal and Tennessee reviewed the trip for Bo and Sonny, describing every facet of their experience to the eager listeners. "Twelve hits of opium for a carton of cigarettes, now that's a hell of a deal," Bo commented.

"They hassled your asses on out of that whore house," Sonny said, laughing. "That's good."

"The look on her face had me convinced," Tennessee said. "She looked like the VC were out there."

"They put on a good act, all right," Hal agreed.

"They didn't want your asses laying around smoking pot and taking up room."

They closed the road and endured radio schedule, while darkness gathered around them. "Tomorrow night Lay's mother is going to cook us a meal," Sonny said.

"That'll be good for a change," Hal said.

"I already paid her so she can buy a chicken at the market tomorrow. So you dudes owe me," Sonny added.

"How much can a chicken cost?" Tennessee asked. "She's over-charging us, man."

"It'll beat C-rats, man. If it's good, maybe we can talk her down on the next meal, like I told you" Sonny said.

"You're such an expert barterer yourself," Hal told Tennessee.

"Well, I'd get her under *that* price," Tennessee replied weakly.

It was late when Sonny, Bo and Tennessee finally turned in, leaving Hal to his double watch. He didn't really mind the long hours ahead of him. He felt absolutely relaxed, and the night held few terrors for him as he sat contemplating the day. It had been as though they had entered a parallel world, one that existed invisible and mostly closed to the Americans. He reveled in their small victory, recalling all they had seen and done, as he watched the stars winking in the heavens.

VI

Hal delayed getting up as long as possible. He lay listening to the muffled sound of traffic and could feel vibrations from the rattling timbers of the bridge. He could smell the dust and knew it was hot outside. The wadded up poncho-liner he used as a pillow was damp from sweat. After finishing his watch he had slept soundly, and now he actually felt refreshed. He sat up and stretched, noting Tennessee's recumbent form across from him. *One less wake-up.* The thought was like a morning mantra. Hal tied his boots, donned his sunglasses, and ventured outside.

"Well, here's sleeping beauty," said Sonny.

"Good morning, gentlemen," Hal said, squinting up at Sonny and Bo. Even with sunglasses, the sunlight was blinding.

"Good afternoon, you mean," Bo said.

"I thought I was going to have to go down there and wake your ass up," said Sonny.

"They got all fucked out in Quin Nhon," Bo said. "They're recuperating."

"Resting up for Bangkok," Hal said.

"You can rest up all you want," Sonny told him. "We're going to Lay's to cool off."

Hal casually heated water for coffee, content to let the day tick on. He put Grand Funk Railroad on the tape-deck and sat drinking coffee. The hot drink started him sweating, however, and he couldn't finish it.

"Damn, it's bright out here," said Tennessee, squinting up at Hal.

"Hot as hell, too. Welcome to Nam," Hal replied.

"Man, I didn't think my watch would ever end," Tennessee said, taking a seat beside Hal.

"It was worth it," Hal said.

"Yesterday was nothing compared to Bangkok," Tennessee said. "We get to Bangkok and we'll stay in a fancy hotel and take hot showers, and smoke some of the best pot in the world. And the best part will be we won't have to worry about some lifer messing with us. It's going to be great."

"We can check out that fish garden, too," Hal added.

"And the massage parlors. One of those guys was telling me about them. You walk in, and it looks like a hotel lobby, with couches and stuffed chairs, fancy carpets. Except there's a huge viewing window displaying a roomful of girls. You sit on a couch and have a drink and select the girl you want. Then she gives you a full massage and bath. If you like her you can take her home. For twenty-five bucks a day she's with you all the time, day and night."

"Subject to your every whim," Hal said wistfully.

"We'll get our own driver, too. When we want to go somewhere, he's right there, waiting."

"We'll live like royalty. Man, I can't wait."

There was a lull in highway traffic, giving them a break from its attendant cacophony and allowing most of the dust to settle.

"Hey, check out that lizard," Tennessee said, pointing across the road.

Hal spotted it, crouched at the edge of the grass across from them. It appeared alert, slowly swinging its head in patient assessment of the road.

"Lizards and snakes—they give me the creeps," Tennessee said. "And this place is full of them."

The lizard, the same reddish color as the dirt, was big. Its thick body was supported on sturdy, muscular legs, and its long tail trailed into the grass.

"I've never seen that kind before," Hal said. He'd always had a fascination for reptiles and amphibians. He had read all of Raymond Ditmar's books on snakes, and as a child had captured countless snakes, lizards, salamanders, frogs, pollywogs, and toads, keeping them as pets until they had either escaped or died. There was a sense of wonder sometimes mixed with fear for a life-form so alien to mammals, one void of human-like emotions but, instead, governed by mystical, primal motivations. Hal got up cautiously and edged to lower ground where he would be out of the lizard's sight.

"What the hell do you think you're doing, man?"

"I'm going to try and catch him," Hal replied.

"Are you nuts? He looks like he'd bite," Tennessee cautioned. Yet he followed Hal to the edge of the road, where they crouched behind a clump of grass. "Now what?" he asked.

"He might be planning to come across to our side," Hal replied. The lizard was posed like a statue, angled away from them. "He does, and I'll grab him when he gets to this side."

"You're crazy! I wouldn't touch that thing with a ten-foot pole."

Suddenly, the lizard jerked as if making up its mind, and started across the road at a trot. Hal waited until it had almost reached their side before he broke from cover and lunged for the animal.

The lizard reacted instantly when it sensed Hal's pursuit, whipping around and reversing direction with surprising speed and agility. Hal had made a good jump, however, and he quickly closed on the fleeing figure.

Looking back at the menacing outstretched hand, the lizard suddenly reared up onto its hind feet. Its body seemed to puff up, and it made a loud hissing sound. The creature accelerated, as if it had changed gears, leaning forward on its hind feet like a runner reaching for the finish line. A ridge on its back, like the dorsal fin of a fish, raised and stood erect.

Hal's attack faltered under this sudden transformation, and his hand jerked back from the lizard. "Damn, did you see that?" he asked.

"Man, it looked like a little fucking dinosaur," Tennessee cried.

"Yeah. Wow, that was something!" Hal said, wiping his hands on his pants.

"You'd better leave that kind of lizard alone, man. They're too weird," Tennessee said.

"No kidding," Hal agreed as they walked back to the bunker. Hal was fascinated by Vietnam's strange variety of wildlife--so different from anything he'd seen at home. But the corridor along the highway had been denuded by defoliants, and offered just a small glimpse of the native wildlife. He could only imagine what animals might lurk in the jungles inland.

Sonny and Bo soon returned from the village. Sonny doctored a Bomber with opium, and they passed it around. "Let's play some cards. I feel lucky," Sonny suggested.

A motorcycle with two Vietnamese slowed as it drew near the bridge and pulled to a stop next to the bunker. The man driving nodded and grinned idiotically beneath huge sunglasses. The woman on the back seat sat side-saddle, her legs crossed and her hat tilted to shade her pretty face. She smiled to them. "What you do?" she asked. Her pants were of a flimsy, translucent material that highlighted her shapely legs.

"What you doing, girl?" Sonny asked.

"We go Phu Cat," the girl replied. "It beaucoup hot," she added, smiling at their admiring stares.

"Me beaucoup hot," said Sonny, taking a long draw on the joint.

"Boom-boom, you," the man told Sonny, nodding and grinning, exhibiting the full extent of his English.

"Soul brodder number one," the girl urged. "Name me, Mai."

The pair on the motorcycle comprised a mobile brothel, one that specialized in servicing Americans guarding bridges along the highway.

"Okay you guys," Sonny said, "why don't you head down to Lay's for awhile. Mai and I have a little business to transact." He gave the man some money and the girl stepped off the motorcycle.

Hal, Tennessee, and Bo followed the man on the motorcycle up the road toward Lay's stand, while Sonny and the girl disappeared inside the bunker.

A cool, damp breeze stirred the trees and blew bits of paper along the ground. The air seemed alive, as though transmitting gossip of impending rain. Dark clouds advancing behind the wind all but confirmed the rumor.

The rain struck before they reached the village. A few big drops pelted them and made craters in the dust, and then they were in the midst of a down-pour. With the smell of wet dirt thick in their nostrils, they started running for the coke stand. By the time they raced under the tarp of Lay's stand, they were soaked.

"Damn! That's some serious rain," Bo shouted over the furious drumming of the raindrops on the canvas above them.

"Hoo-eee! I mean to tell you," Tennessee yelled in agreement.

Lay was laughing and shouting at her two little sisters, who were jumping in and out of the rain, their screams muffled by the chaos of the driving torrent.

Hal shook water from his arms and looked around at the others: the motorcycle driver, huddled and smiling at the children; Bo and Tennessee, shouting encouragement; and Lay, half-heartedly trying to restore order, all bonded by this refuge from nature's fury. A jeep passed, going slow through the downpour, its windshield wipers slapping back and forth. Kids gathered around a puddle next to the road. Naked, they took turns running through the puddle, splashing water and shouting, their cries of excitement all but lost in the storm's uproar.

When the rain passed as suddenly as it had appeared, the assemblage remained huddled, as if stunned by the recent violence. Lay served cold drinks, and they sat listening to the musical toll of running water that dripped from the canvas roof, the trees and house gutters.

"You beaucoup wet. Same-same baby-san," Lay teased the Americans, pointing to the children jumping in the puddle.

The sun broke free of the clouds, and bright rainbows arced across the sky. In the storm's aftermath, the village returned to a hushed tranquility. Most of the population was working in the fields, and the village was nearly deserted.

"Your mother cooks for us tonight, hey?" Hal asked Lay.

"Yes, she cook for you. I bring to you."

"Good. Number one," Hal said, nodding his head and smiling. He relished the prospect of a good home-cooked meal--a novelty from the normal canned food.

The motorcycle driver fired up his machine and started toward the bridge. Hal, Tennessee, and Bo followed leisurely behind. When they got to the bridge the motorcycle was pulling away with both its occupants, and Sonny was pacing back toward the bunker.

"You get your money's worth?" Bo asked.

"That was great in that rain," Sonny declared.

"Another satisfied customer," Tennessee said.

"Best piece of ass I've had in a long time."

"She's probably hit every bridge between here and Danang," Bo said.

"Good, then Cathcart gets my sloppy seconds." Sonny painted some Bombers with opium and they sat on the bunker, smoking and letting the sun dry their uniforms.

"The two VC are gone," Sonny said.

"What do you mean gone?" asked Hal.

"Bo and I walked down there earlier and they were just finishing burying them. They'd just rolled them off a few feet and stuck them in a hole."

"Man, that would sure suck," said Tennessee.

"I bet they were getting ripe," Hal said.

A few children gathered at the bridge, signaling time to open the swimming hole. Bo dropped a grenade into the pool, and the children cheered when the water exploded high into the air. There followed a scramble for the water, and the pool was soon animated by the waves of splashing bodies. Hal and Sonny bobbed in the murky water like guests at a spa, while Bo grabbed and flung little squirming pirates into the depths.

After a lengthy session in the healing waters, the GIs sat on the bunker, smoking and watching the afternoon dwindle. The highway grew quiet, and the dust settled wearily after its day-long bout.

"It's been quiet from the Hill," Bo said.

"Don't complain. Those boys are busy," Sonny said, laughing.

"Yeah, we could see them up there stringing barbed wire when we went by," Hal said.

"It keeps them out of our hair, at least," Sonny said.

"Yeah, you can't over-estimate the importance of perimeter security," Hal agreed.

"I can't wait for mama-san's meal," Sonny said, looking eagerly toward the village.

"I'm getting damn hungry, I know that," Bo said. "I hope it isn't too weird."

"It'll be great," Sonny assured him. "Real Vietnamese food, man."

They pulled the wire across the road, policed the area, and got their mess kits out.

"Here comes supper," Hal finally announced.

They looked down the road and could see Lay, Tuan, and Tim approaching.

"All right, I'm starving," Sonny said.

Lay and Tuan carried large ceramic bowls with metal lids to keep the food warm. "We have food for you," Lay said.

"It number one," said Tuan, as the soldiers converged around the bowls.

The larger bowl held rice, and in the other bowl was an aromatic greenish sauce with chunks of chicken in it.

"It smells good," Hal said, as they dug into the food.

"It tastes great," said Sonny after taking a bite. "Number one," he told Lay.

"How, what name me?" Tuan asked Hal.

"You name Tommy," Hal answered.

"What name me?" Tim asked.

"You name Timmy."

The boys laughed, apparently satisfied. "How, me play?" Tuan asked, and Hal gave him the harmonica. "What name this?" Tuan asked him.

"It's a harmonica," Hal replied. "You'll never be able to say that, though. It's a harp. A harp."

"Hop," said Tuan, nodding.

"Close enough," Hal said with a laugh.

Tuan blew on the harmonica, experimenting with the sounds it could produce.

"This is good," Bo said, his mouth full of food.

"It's beyond good, man. This is far out," Tennessee said.

"Hey, ease up on that racket, Tommy," Sonny told Tuan, who was blowing as hard as he could on the harmonica. "I'm trying to eat."

"Tell mama-san food number one," Hal told Lay.

Lay received the compliments with a graceful smile and held the bowls out to them for seconds.

"You same-same water buffalo. You eat beaucoup," Tim told Bo, slapping him on the arm and quickly retreating.

Bo made a lunge for Tim, upsetting Sonny's plate.

"Damn, you're as bad as the kids," Sonny cried, looking down at the spilled food.

"There wasn't much left on your plate, Bo," Bo said, laughing with the children.

Lay spooned the last of the food onto Sonny's plate. "It getting dark," she said, gathering up the bowls. "We go home."

"Yeah, VC come for you," Bo said.

"VC come for *you*," Tim countered.

"VC come, I cocky-dow. I show you," Bo said, his menacing bulk beginning to rise, impelling Tim to dart away.

"Tell your mother food number one," Sonny told Lay.

"Number one," Hal agreed.

"Maybe she cook for us again in one week," Sonny said.

"Okay, I say to her," Lay replied, and she led Tuan and Tim back to the village.

"Now that's what I call some good eating," Sonny said.

"She's still charging us too much," Tennessee said.

"So I'll talk her down some on the next meal, man. This was kind of a test run."

Hal blew softly on the harmonica while the daylight faded.

"We're getting low on water. We need to send some jugs in," Sonny said.

"I look for Mimms to show up tomorrow," Bo said.

"Yeah, maybe they need more sandbags up on the Hill," Sony said and laughed.

After an interlude of talk and joking, Hal was once again alone on the bunker. He sat with ears attuned to the night's subtle noises, while his mind soared and grappled with life's complexities.

VII

"A jeep," Bo said the next morning, after they had just finished their first Bomber and were sitting drinking coffee.

They watched the military jeep speeding toward them from the south, and as it drew nearer they could make out the heads of three passengers.

"It's the Hill," Tennessee said.

"Yeah, and Martin," Sonny said.

They made a quick check to be sure nothing incriminating was laying out in sight.

"The lieutenant is with them, too," Tennessee said, as the jeep drew yet closer.

The jeep crossed the bridge and pulled to a stop in front of them. Lieutenant Edmonds sat in front next to Mimms, and Sergeant Martin sat in the back. "You men are *slobs*!" Sergeant Martin said in greeting. He and the lieutenant got out of the jeep.

"When was the last time this perimeter was cleared of brush?" Lieutenant Edmonds asked.

"I don't know exactly, sir," Sonny answered, looking out at the grass and clumps of weeds growing amidst the barbed wire.

"That's right, Jones. You have no idea because it was so long ago," Sergeant Martin said. "This perimeter is a disgrace!"

Lieutenant Edmonds and Sergeant Martin went into the bunker, accompanied by Sonny. Hal noted that Martin carried a notebook and pencil. Hal shook his head and exchanged looks of doom with Tennessee.

The inspection team emerged from the bunker. Sonny trailed behind the sergeant and lieutenant with downcast, weary eyes. "It should be a few days before we can get the barbed wire," Lieutenant Edmonds was saying. "We can get a timetable on that from HQ. But we should be able to get you some sandbags today." He spoke with animation and seemed excited about the project.

Mimms was sitting in the jeep, smiling gleefully at the proceedings. When he saw Hal and Tennessee looking at him, he winked. They could only glare at him in helpless fury.

"You can start by clearing the perimeter," Lieutenant Edmonds continued. "We'll pick up machetes and shovels for you."

Sonny nodded silently.

Sergeant Martin put the notebook back into his pocket and lit his half-burned cigar. "You guys think you're on vacation down here," he said. He heaved himself into the jeep and plopped into the back seat. "From now on it's going to be a working vacation," he said and smiled triumphantly.

Hal and Tennessee loaded the empty water cans into the jeep and stood rigidly, watching the vehicle pull away and motor down the road toward LZ English and battalion headquarters.

"Oh man, what the fuck? We've got to do the whole perimeter?" Bo cried.

"That's not all," Sonny said. "They want us to re-build the bunker, too."

"What?" Tennessee fumed, beginning to pace. "Oh man, I don't believe this shit."

"What's wrong with the bunker?" Hal asked.

"It don't matter, man," Sonny replied. "That fucking cherry lieutenant, all he knows is the book."

"All those sandbags! Oh man," said Bo, and he kicked savagely at the bunker.

"You guys are on a working vacation now. Fuck you, Martin." Tennessee, said. "Fuck you, Martin!" he yelled at the top of his voice at the now empty highway.

Sonny dug his opium bottle out from under some sandbags, and he dabbed black streaks onto Bombers. He passed the joints out, and they sat on the bunker, smoking somberly.

"Fucking lifers," Bo fussed.

"I knew things were going too good to last," Sonny said.

"Hey, we don't have to fill any sandbags," said Hal.

"What are you talking about? You heard what they said," Tennessee said harshly, as if resentful of any doubt about the total disaster facing them.

"We just take the old sandbags and put them in the new ones they bring us. We tie them up, and they'll never know the difference," Hal said.

"That's a brilliant idea," Sonny said. "I like it."

"Yeah, the hell with filling more sandbags," Bo said.

"We still have to rebuild the damn thing," Tennessee said. "And do the whole perimeter."

They sat looking at the concertina-wire strewn perimeter as though it were the enemy, smoking and mulling over thoughts in silence.

"We might as well play some spades," Sonny finally said. "We can't do anything until they bring us the shovels and sandbags."

"It might be a while before we have the time to play cards again," Bo said.

"I guess so," said Tennessee. "It beats sitting here, thinking about what a dumb slob Martin is."

Hal was left on duty as the others went down into the bunker. He put a cassette into the tape-deck and settled into his seat. Soon he could hear the sounds of argument and laughter from inside the bunker.

A jeep with long whip-antennas followed by armored MP vehicles, the lead elements of a large convoy, passed, and Hal steeled himself for the coming dust storm. Trucks, jeeps, tanks and armored personnel carriers ground past in an endless train. Hal huddled against the maelstrom, bandanna pulled over his nose and mouth, and gazed into the pall of dust. He plugged in the head-phone and endured the monotonous procession.

After the convoy had finally passed, Tennessee came out to relieve Hal. "You're quite a sight," Tennessee said, laughing.

"Damn, that was the biggest convoy I've seen yet," Hal said. "What a fucking mess." He rinsed the dirt from his upper body and went into the bunker. "Are you guys still into playing some cards?" he asked.

"We're waiting for you, man," Sonny said.

"Let's play some hearts," Hal suggested.

"Oh man, I always get the damn queen," Bo said.

"Then it's pay-back time, baby," said Sonny. "I'm getting burned out on spades anyways."

"Oh okay, we'll try some hearts, then," Bo said, and he dealt the cards.

Hal and Sonny delighted at Bo's rising irritation as the game progressed. "Damn!" Bo cried, slamming both fists down on the table.

Hal and Sonny were laughing hysterically. "Damn, Bo, you almost ran them all, except for that one heart," Sonny said. Tears were streaming from his eyes.

"You guys did that on purpose, didn't you?"" Bo accused them.

"No! Hell, we thought you were trying to run them," Hal sputtered.

They were interrupted by Tennessee's call, "Incoming. Front and center!"

"It must be Martin," Sonny said soberly, wiping the tears from his face.

"Great," Bo said. "This will make my day complete."

The jeep had already stopped, and Tennessee was walking toward it. "Look at Martin stuffed in the back. He looks like Santa Claus," Hal whispered as they slowly moved toward the jeep.

"Santa Claus from hell," Sonny said.

"What's so damn funny, Doyle?" Martin asked.

"Nothing Sergeant," Bo replied.

"Well, I have some things here that you'll get a real kick out of," Sergeant Martin said. "Here Knox," he said, and he handed Tennessee two shovels and two machetes. Meanwhile, Sonny and Hal grabbed the filled water cans and carried them to the bunker.

"We didn't have room for *all* the sandbags, but we brought you a few to get you started," Sergeant Martin told them, and he dropped a stack of empty bags onto the ground. He pointed out to the perimeter and said, "Now I don't want to see so much as a blade of grass out there."

"Airborne, Sergeant!" Bo barked with vehemence.

"That's the spirit Doyle," Sergeant Martin said, smiling and chomping on his cigar. "Let's get the rest of this stuff to Bridge Eleven. They'll be waiting for us," he told Mimms.

"What an ass," Hal said after the jeep had crossed the bridge.

"No wonder they couldn't fit all the sandbags in there, with his fat ass in the back," Tennessee said.

"Well boys, I guess we have no choice," Sonny said.

They took turns with the machetes, hacking at the stubborn weeds. Hal looked out to the rice paddies, where villagers were wielding their implements of harvest. As he toiled under the sun's glare, he tried to draw a parallel in their undertaking. But the similarity was superficial. For where the Vietnamese were actually reaping something of value, the Americans were merely reducing the perimeter to the barren earth of military preference.

When they had finished the detail, they made a bee-line for the swimming hole. They gladly slid into the water, letting the heat and grime wash from their bodies.

"Bangkok's looking better all the time, man," Hal told Tennessee.

"ETS sounds even better. Fuck the Army," Tennessee said.

"You got an attitude problem, baby," Sonny said. "It don't mean nothing, man."

"Yeah right, it don't mean nothing," Tennessee said bitterly.

They returned to the bunker and went about their mechanical preparations for supper. Hal and Tennessee pulled the wire across the road, symbolically drawing another day to a close.

"God damn!" Tennessee cursed, walking back to the bunker and buttoning his pants. "I think I've got the clap," he announced.

"It's got a runny nose?" Bo asked, laughing.

"Very funny, man," Tennessee said.

"You thought it was pretty funny when I got it."

"This is just great!" Tennessee said.

Sonny stopped laughing long enough to say, "So you get a free ride to English and get a shot of penicillin. No big deal, man."

"Yeah, sure. Martin's going to hassle me. I can hear him now: 'How could you possibly catch clap if you were at your post?' Damn, R and R just days away, too."

"I hope I don't get it," Hal said, his hand involuntarily cupping his crotch.

"Fuck it. Let's take a walk to the village. I need to stretch my legs," Sonny said.

"I'm not going anywhere," Tennessee said with finality. "Anyways, I've got a letter to write."

"Dear mom, I didn't think it would happen to me," Bo said.

"Ha-ha Doyle, very fucking funny," Tennessee said.

They walked to the village, leaving Tennessee at the bunker, sourly toking on a Bomber. The children were once again massed on the road, gathered in laughing, singing groups.

"Hey man, where you go?" Tuan asked them.

"Tommy! What's happening?" said Sonny.

Tuan beamed, and Thieu and Tim drew up beside him.

"Timmy and Billy!" Bo said, and the boys laughed and nodded.

"You work beaucoup. I see you," said Thieu. "Same-same work in rice," he said, and he bent over and made hacking motions with his arm.

"Yeah, we work beaucoup, thanks to the damn lifers," Bo said.

"Lifahs number ten," agreed Tuan.

"Your mother's cooking number one," Sonny said.

"Yes, we like very much," Hal agreed.

"You say to her?" Tuan asked, motioning to the entrance to his family's house.

"Okay, we come thank your mother," Sonny said, nodding his head.

They followed Tuan into the darker shadows of the trees. Tuan's mother and father were sitting on the front porch, and his two little sisters were playing on the floor at their father's feet. They looked up and smiled when they saw the Americans. Tuan's father was a distinguished looking man, tall for a

97

Vietnamese, with hair graying around the temples. His smile looked weary but friendly.

"Mama-san, food last night number one," Sonny said.

Tuan interpreted for his mother, and they all smiled and laughed. "She say, maybe you want she cook more for you," Tuan said.

"Yes, we want."

"You say when, and she cook for you."

"Okay, very good."

"How, me play hop for father me?" Tuan asked Hal.

"Sure Tommy," Hal replied, and he gave Tuan the harmonica.

Tuan blew vigorously on the instrument, demonstrating its full range of sounds. His parents laughed, shaking their heads when he hit a particularly obnoxious note.

Sonny looked up at the darkening sky after Tuan had finished his concert. "Well, I guess we'd better get back," he said.

They said good night to Tuan's parents and walked back to the highway. Bats fluttered and dove from the trees as they walked down the road. They waded through frolicking children, answering their greetings with a waving of hands, like priests granting blessings. They returned to their stark outpost and shuffled about, preparing for nightfall.

"You didn't talk the mama-san down on her price?" Tennessee asked Sonny.

"It didn't seem like the time, with her husband there and all. Don't worry, man. I'll get it straight with her."

"I hope so. We're getting ripped off."

"Relax, man. We've got just sixteen more days until R and R," Hal told Tennessee.

"Yeah, and all I can think about is getting rid of this damn clap. What if I have it while we're on R and R, like Mimms? I'm going to keep it in my pants until we get to Bangkok."

"That would be a good idea," Hal agreed.

"You don't feel anything yet?" Tennessee asked.

"No, I don't have it," Hal replied. He had inspected his penis three times during the course of the afternoon and had urinated with a dread of the tell-tale pain, but his fears had thus far been groundless.

"I hope they don't bring the barbed wire tomorrow," Bo said.

"Nah, they won't be able to get it tomorrow. But they are going to pick up more sandbags," Sonny said.

"That'll be great," Tennessee said. "I can't wait."

"We know what to do with them. It won't be bad, man," Sonny said.

"We'll have those sandbags filled so fast, it'll blow Martin's mind," Bo vowed.

"No, we'd better milk it. We finish up too fast and Martin will get suspicious or come up with something else for us to do," Hal cautioned.

They smoked and talked into the night, their discussions ranging from the Hill to home. Finally, Sonny rose, saying, "It's time for me to hit the sack, man."

Bo and Tennessee got up and moved off to urinate. "Very funny, man," Tennessee was saying to Bo, and then their voices became muffled as they entered the bunker.

Hal was left alone to his shift., He knew that in the later hours there would be a sliver of moon to lend a bit of illumination, but there was no hint of its appearance yet. He peered into the darkness and gradually relaxed, letting his mind wander. People's faces flashed through his memory, friends and relatives, a mixed gallery ranging back to grade school. He replayed events from the past and contemplated his future. The nine months he'd been in-county felt like nine years, creating a gulf that dimmed his past and made the future uncertain.

Hal looked down at his watch. His shift was nearly over, and he was calculating when to start waking Tennessee, when he heard a sound, a soft metallic pinging noise. He raised his head, trying to analyze the sound and realized that it was something striking the perimeter's concertina wire. Just then the ground erupted in a tremendous explosion. Red sparks and streamers filled the darkness, like a fountain of fire. The light was blinding, numbing. Hal could see his hands gripping the sandbags, like in a snap-shot.

"What the fuck?" Sonny shouted from inside the bunker.

Hal grabbed his M-16 and began firing blindly into the renewed darkness in the direction of the original sound.

Sonny, Bo, and Tennessee scrambled out of the bunker and clawed their way onto the top. "What happened?" Sonny gasped.

"I didn't see shit!" Hal cried.

"Bo, get on the M-60," Sonny said. "I'm going to pop a flare." Sonny fumbled in the darkness, and then the flare shot up into the sky and burst into light.

The landscape looked ghostly in the stark light. For some crazy reason it reminded Hal of night skiing. They could see nothing moving in the scene before them.

"I heard something from down there, near the creek," Hal told them, pointing.

"Shoot it up, Bo," Sonny said.

Bo opened up with the machine-gun. They watched the tracers spray the brush as the flare above them rode gently down on its parachute.

A shot whined over their heads, and then another round struck a sandbag. Hal could see the muzzle flashes from the tree-line near the village. "From the village," he hissed.

They shifted around to survey the tree-line in the expiring light of the flare. "Be damn sure of your target," Sonny reminded them. "There's houses over there."

Sonny fired another flare, and the tree-line stood illuminated under the renewed light. The shadows surrounding the trees were impenetrable, however, and they couldn't detect any movement.

"*Eagle-three, this is Eagle-one. What's going on down there? Over.*"

Sonny grabbed the microphone. "Eagle-one, this is Eagle-three. We're being hit!" he yelled. "We're taking some sniper fire from the tree-line to our north, over."

"*Roger Eagle-three. Stand by.*"

They crouched, struggling to hear above the noises of their breathing. But the only sounds they could hear were the barking of dogs from the village. Bo fired another burst from the M-60 at the creek, but there was no reaction or signs of fleeing sappers.

Hal noticed something red rise into the air above the Hill. He watched with growing curiosity as it arced slowly toward them. Just when he realized that it was coming their way, it zoomed over their heads. Another red spark took to the air, and another, and there were rounds spinning over their heads and thudding into the ground around them.

"Jesus Christ, they're shooting at us!" Tennessee shouted.

Sonny scrambled for the radio. "Eagle-one, this is Eagle-three. Cease firing! You're shooting at us, damn it!" He shouted into the microphone.

"*Eagle-three, Eagle-one. Say again? Over.*"

"Quit shooting at us, you mother fuckers!"

"*Roger, roger. Stand by. Over.*""

"Shit! Those were fifty-caliber rounds," Sonny said.

"Those dumb bastards!" Bo cursed.

"I don't know who's worse, the VC or those assholes on the Hill," Hal said.

"That's great! We get shot by our own guys. That sounds about right," Tennessee said.

They could hear two shots from somewhere in the village, but they were distant and not directed at them. There was a rising chorus of barking, and they could hear shouting.

"Eagle-three, Eagle-one, over."

They could recognize the voice of Lieutenant Edmonds on the radio now.

"Eagle-one, Eagle-three, over." Sonny replied.

"Eagle-three, give me a status report, over."

"Roger, Eagle-one. It's quiet here at the moment, but we just heard a couple of shots from the village. Over."

"Roger, Eagle-three. Just stay put and stand by. Over."

"Roger, roger. Eagle-three standing by."

"The dumb shit. Where in the fuck does he think we're going to go?" Tennessee scoffed.

"I'll bet it was that dumb-ass Lieutenant that had them shoot us up," Bo said.

Another shot rang out from the village, followed by shouts and screams.

"Whatever's going on, it doesn't sound good," Hal said.

"Eagle-three, this is Eagle-one, over."

"Eagle-one, Eagle-three. There's something going on in the village. We hear shots and some shouting, over."

"Roger, Eagle-three. Just sit tight. Casper is sending two gun-ships your way, over."

"Roger Eagle-one. Eagle-three standing by."

The shouting had given way to wailing and screams of agony. "It sounds like they're torturing somebody," Bo said.

Hal thought of the Lay and Lin, Tuan and Tim, and the terror that was stalking them while they hunkered helplessly on their bunker."This really sucks, man," he said bitterly.

"I know, man, but what do you want to do? Go running in there like the cavalry?" Sonny asked. "We can't see shit. So just be cool and wait for the gunships."

They listened and waited, firing another flare when the light started to falter. The cries from the village dwindled to an occasional agonizing appeal. They listened intently, but as the minutes passed the night grew still, disturbed only by the periodic bark of a dog.

"Listen! I hear choppers," Sonny said.

Hal could hear the distant "whop-whop" of the helicopters, rapidly gaining in volume, and then they could see them, two cobra gun-ships, sleek as barracudas, advancing over the treetops.

The helicopters split up, each taking a side of the village, and then they opened fire with their mini-guns, saturating the area surrounding the village and bridge with rounds. The solid streams of tracers licked the ground from the gun-ships' beaked noses, emitting a roar like a dragon growling. It seemed impossible that any living thing could escape the waves of destruction being wrought by these predatory machines.

"Any VC out there, and they're toast," Tennessee said, as they watched the impressive light display.

"They're gone, man. The VC already booked," Sonny said.

"The war of attrition at its finest," Hal said, awed by the violence.

When the helicopters had spent their ammunition, they whirred off into the night like futuristic robots.

After the chaos of the past hour, the ensuing silence was profound. The dogs had even ceased their barking. The soldiers sat nervously still, their ears ringing. When their last flare fizzed out, the area returned to darkness.

"It's so damn dark, it's like looking into a well," Bo said.

"Well, whoever was out there, ain't there no more," Sonny said.

They slowly relaxed, yet there was no thought of going back to sleep.

"It must have been a satchel charge," Sonny said. "One of them must have snuck up the creek and then thrown it from near the edge of the perimeter."

"It's a damn good thing he didn't have a very good arm," Tennessee said.

"It probably hit the wire. That must have been what I heard," Hal said.

"That cherry Lieutenant came closer to killing us than the VC," Tennessee said.

"I don't *even* want to think about what a fifty-cal would do to your body," Hal said.

"I've seen it. You don't want to know, man. It ain't pretty, man," Sonny said.

"I wonder what went on in the village," Hal said.

"I don't know, man. It didn't sound good," Tennessee said.

"We'll have to wait for morning to find out, my friend," Sonny said.

"It doesn't seem like we did much of a job protecting the village from the VC, just sitting here," Hal said. "Damn, this really sucks."

They maintained an hourly radio schedule with the Hill and passed the quiet hours talking softly, reviewing the night's events.

VIII

With the first graying of light they could hear the jeep coming. The adrenalin of the attack had long since subsided, and they were merely glad the night was finally over. They roused themselves from their nests when the jeep drew near the bridge. Rushing forward, they pulled the wire back from the road, and the jeep advanced slowly with headlights extinguished.

The jeep rolled across the bridge bearing four passengers. Along with Mimms, Sergeant Martin and Lieutenant Edmunds, was Day, from Bridge Eleven. All four wore steel helmets that wobbled atop their heads.

"What's the situation?" Lieutenant Edmonds asked when the jeep stopped next to the bunker.

"It's been quiet," Sonny replied.

"We'll await full daylight," Lieutenant Edmonds said, as the four disembarked from the jeep.

Sonny recreated the night's events, pointing to the perimeter where the charge had exploded, and to the tree-line where the snipers had been.

"And we took some friendly fire there, there, and there," Tennessee added, pointing to the ground around them.

Sergeant Martin glared with lips tightened, but didn't respond.

Once daylight had advanced, Sergeant Martin said, "Jones, you and Henly will come with us, so get your helmets and weapons."

"Brigade is sending an interpreter down," Lieutenant Edmonds told them.

"A company of ARVNs will do a sweep, too, and check for any kills," Sergeant Martin added.

Hal and Sonny gathered their equipment and were soon ready.

"Okay, let's move out," Lieutenant Edmonds said.

Sergeant Martin turned to Bo, saying, "You guys can do a sweep of the perimeter."

Tennessee nudged Hal. "You look like a turtle under that helmet," he whispered, laughing at the ungainly steel pot wobbling on Hal's head.

"Ha, ha," Hal replied, and he turned to follow the entourage toward the village. Lieutenant Edmonds led the slowly walking figures, their helmets heaving and wobbling like camels' humps.

The village, partially hidden in the trees, was silent and seemingly deserted, like it had been sucked clean of every living thing. Normally, the boys would be herding the cattle out to pasture, but they were nowhere to be seen. As the soldiers drew nearer to the houses, however, Hal could see first one then another occupant furtively watching them from windows and front porches.

Tim approached the Americans from his house. Gone was the energetic spring in his step when he normally greeted them. Instead, he seemed frightened, reluctant. "VC come," he told them with eyes wide and wet with tears. "VC come!" he said with rising agitation. "VC come, they shoot." Tim's excitement grew, and he spoke rapidly in Vietnamese.

"Whoa, whoa, Tim," Sonny said, trying to calm him. "Tell us what happen."

"VC, they come. They shoot father Tuan," Tim cried, tears streaming down his face.

"You show us," Lieutenant Edmonds urged.

Tim led them to Tuan's house. The front porch was crowded with people, and Hal could hear crying from inside. The mourners parted, and the towering, ungainly soldiers followed Tim into the equally crowded interior. The room smelled of incense and burning wax from candles. Tuan's father was laid out on a blanket spread over a table. He looked peaceful and unblemished, as if asleep rather than dead. A cloth was wrapped around his head to hide the bullet wound.

When Tuan's mother saw them, her crying rose in pitch. She spoke in rapid sobs, advancing toward them. By the time she had reached Lieutenant Edmonds, she was screaming hysterically. She hit him with closed fists, up and down, like she was using a tomahawk.

Lieutenant Edmonds backed into the others, recoiling from the attack. He held his arms out to protect himself. His glasses had fallen awry and hung sideways on his head. But the frail blows rained upon the hulking American sounded like hollow, impotent smacks.

Most of the adults were unfamiliar to Hal, and that added to the scene's strangeness. But he did know Tuan, Lay, Lin and the other kids. He didn't have an answer to their questioning looks of condemnation, however.

A relative guided Tuan's mother back to her seat, but the other villagers began to speak rapidly, like they, too, had caught the fever of her anguish.

The five soldiers backed out the door and through the throng outside. Some South Vietnamese military personnel were approaching from the road, and they walked to meet them.

Straightening his glasses, Lieutenant Edmonds talked briefly with the Vietnamese soldiers. He turned to his men. "The interpreter has arrived," he told them. "So, back to the bridge, men. They can take it from here. We've learned all we need to know."

They filed back to the road, and Hal took one last look at the house, where the interpreter's severe voice seemed to have quelled the hysteria.

Tennessee, Bo and Mimms awaited them expectantly. "What's the story?" Tennessee asked.

"The VC executed Lay and Tuan's father," Sonny replied bitterly.

"No shit! Oh man!" Tennessee said, shaking his head.

"How's Lay and Tuan and the family taking it?" Bo asked.

"Mama-san, she's screaming, and the kids are all crying, and the rest of the villagers are yelling and jabbering. It's a crazy scene, man."

"They just dragged him out of their house and shot him," Hal said.

"Mimms, you run Day back to Bridge Eleven and come back for us," Sergeant Martin said. "We'll have to make a report to Battalion."

The jeep left with Mimms and Day, and the others waited beside the bunker.

"Why'd the VC kill him?" Tennessee asked.

"According to the Vietnamese, it has something to do with the rice harvest," Lieutenant Edmonds said. "If a village doesn't give the VC their quota of rice, they've been executing the village chief."

When the jeep returned, Tennessee approached Lieutenant Edmonds, saying, "Sir, I need to go in to the clinic."

"What you need to go to the clinic for?" Sergeant Martin asked.

"I need a shot of penicillin."

"Don't tell me you've got a case of the clap," Sergeant Martin said, hands on hips.

"It looks that way," Tennessee answered contritely.

"And just how do you get clap if you're at your post, Knox?" asked Sergeant Martin.

"I don't know. Maybe it was a mosquito."

"Very funny. Get your ass in the back seat," Sergeant Martin commanded.

Tennessee jumped into the back of the jeep, shrinking to the far side when Sergeant Martin climbed in beside him. "While we're gone, you guys can start filling sandbags," Sergeant Martin told the others. "When you finish with these, there's more where they came from," he added with a savage smile.

"Airborne, asshole," Hal said after the jeep had left. "I pity Tennessee having to sit next to that fat-ass all the way back to English."

"Mimms says it was the lieutenant that had Metzger shoot up the muzzle-flashes," Bo told them.

"I knew it. That dumb shit!" Sonny said.

"All in all, another lovely day in the army," Hal said.

Sonny doled out joints and they sat smoking dejectedly.

Hal spotted groups of ARVNs slowly walking the paddy dikes, executing their sweep.

"I bet they won't find shit," Sonny said.

Hal's gaze kept returning to the village, where life seemed to be slowly recovering. Several Vietnamese police, the "white mice," loitered in the road.

The three boys drove the cattle across the bridge, but they exhibited a studied indifference to the soldiers as they passed.

"Now we're the bad guys," Hal said.

"What do they expect?" Bo asked.

"We sat here and did nothing," Hal said. "That's all they know."

"And the VC are the good guys, according to all the anti-war assholes," Tennessee said. "They torture and kill just for the hell of it."

"Who knows the real reason? Shit, these people have been going at it for thirty years or more, man. They've got all kinds of feuds and shit," Sonny said.

The pulse of the highway picked up, but the trucks rattling the bridge hardly drew their notice as they surveyed the village, trying to digest the night's action. The company of ARVNs had completed their sweep and were assembling and loading onto trucks.

"I bet they didn't find shit," Bo said.

"Yeah man, those VC were long gone before the choppers ever got here," Sonny agreed.

Once the ARVN trucks had pulled away, the village seemed to take on a semblance of normalcy. Farmers were filtering out into the rice paddies, the sun's intensity began to build, and the highway's dust started to rise into its customary cloud.

"Well, we'd better knock off these sandbags before Martin gets back," Sonny finally said.

"There can't be more than fifty here," Bo said, looking down at the stack of new bags. "That shouldn't take us long."

"We might as well make it look good and fill these bags. We can do our thing with the old ones after they bring the rest of the bags," Sonny said.

"The good thing is, they won't have room in the jeep to bring them on this trip," Hal said.

Hal and Bo took up the shovels and dug into the bank near the bridge, while Sonny held the sandbags. They accepted the project almost gratefully, glad to submerge their minds in physical labor. Sonny stacked the filled sandbags into a neat pile next to the bunker.

The jeep returned later in the afternoon and deposited Tennessee. Sergeant Martin untied a bundle of sandbags lashed to the vehicle's frame and tossed it to the ground. "We didn't have a lot of room, but I knew you'd want a few to keep you busy," he said. He regained his seat, and the jeep continued on to the Hill in a huff of dust.

"Get all fixed up?" Bo asked Tennessee.

"Yeah, yeah. I got a shot in the ass. I also had to sit next to Martin all the way to English and listen to his shit. Man, what an ass!"

They stood glaring down at the bundle of sandbags. "Well, dudes, let's get this over with," Sonny finally said.

They grabbed the shovels and returned to their quarry. They took turns holding the bags and shoveling, working with a savage aggression.

There were no children at the swimming hole that afternoon, and Hal and Sonny floated the unusually quiet water atop their air mattresses.

"It seems like we should do something," Hal said.

"They're probably having a funeral procession and what not. We'd best not intrude right now."

"I guess you're right. I'm feeling pretty shitty, though."

"Aren't we all," Sonny said.

They spent a subdued evening on the bunker, enduring tense but uneventful night watches.

IX

The three boys drove the cattle from the village at the accustomed hour. Hal smiled and waved as they passed, but again, the boys refused to look at the Americans. They prodded the cattle with sticks to hurry them past the bunker, their faces set and stern.

There was no further contact with the village as the day wound on: no Tuan, Tim or Thieu stopping by to banter; no kids coming to swim. The silence from the village was matched by that from the Hill. They passed the day glancing furtively, first toward the village, then up the road to the Hill. Only the traffic remained unchanged, grinding by in its endless procession and reestablishing its thick atmosphere of dust.

"I thought they were all hot for us to do this bunker," Tennessee said, when the expected jeep from the Hill failed to materialize.

"Don't complain, man. I'm not in any hurry to rebuild the damn bunker," Sonny replied.

"We'll see them tomorrow. That's soon enough," Bo said.

"Yeah, tomorrow's mail day," Hal agreed.

"And hot chow," Tennessee added.

"I wonder if we'll get any customers from the village," Hal said.

"Yeah," Bo said doubtfully.

After supper Sonny suggested they walk to the village. "We've got to break the ice some time," he said.

"You guys go ahead," Bo said. "I wouldn't know what to say."

"There's not much we *can* say," Sonny said. "Hell, we feel bad, too. That's all we can say."

Hal and Tennessee walked with Sonny to the village. The children were playing in the street, like on any other evening. As they approached the children, however, Hal sensed a reserve in their play and a more circumspect demeanor. There were no waves of greeting or two fingers held up in a peace-sign. The Americans walked the gauntlet of children, smiling awkwardly, until they saw Tuan standing with Tim.

"Tommy," Sonny said in greeting.

Tuan didn't laugh or smile at them. "VC, they kill father me," he said.

"We're sorry, Tommy," Sonny replied.

"Why you no come? We call for you. You no come," Tuan said, his face contorted into a fury that resembled hatred.

An old lady scowled at them as she savagely swept her dirt yard with a short scimitar-shaped broom.

"We couldn't leave the bridge. They were shooting at us, too," Sonny said.

"The lifers say we must stay at the bridge," Hal added.

"Ha!" Tuan scoffed. "You afraid of VC." He turned and walked rapidly away from them.

"Tommy," Sonny called, but Tuan didn't stop. Sonny turned to Tim. "Timmy, there wasn't anything we could do." But Tim turned away from them and ran to catch up with Tuan.

The children had stopped playing and stood watching the Americans. A sense of impotence and anguish washed over Hal. As they walked back to the bridge, he felt stiff and alien.

"Damn, it's not our fault they killed him," Bo said.

"They figure we should have done something," Sonny said with a sigh.

"Damn! Whatever happens, we're always the fuck-ups. I'm tired of this shit," Tennessee said.

"Man, I can't wait for R and R," Hal said. Two weeks, however, seemed like an eternity.

They smoked their Bombers, observing a moody silence, and drifted apart to write letters for the next day's out-going mail. They took their turns at guard duty, taking some heart in the gradual ascendancy of the moon over the darkness.

The next morning, just after they had drawn the concertina wire from the road to usher in another day, they noted a jeep approaching from the south.

"Watch your joints," Sonny told them. They snubbed their joints and slid them under sandbags and then lifted their cups and sipped coffee until the jeep arrived.

"Good morning gentlemen. Any out-going mail?" Lieutenant Edmonds asked.

"Good morning sir," Sonny replied, and he handed the lieutenant the sack of letters.

"I hope nobody else needs to see the medics," Sergeant Martin said, looking hard at Tennessee. "I see you got a start on filling those sandbags," he added, motioning to the stack of newly-filled bags.

"Yeah, we filled all we had," Sonny replied.

"Well, hold off on that for now. There might be a change of plans," Sergeant Martin told them.

"A change of plans?" Sonny asked.

"We'll know more after we talk to Battalion," Lieutenant Edmonds said.

"Now just what the hell did *that* mean?" Tennessee asked after the jeep had departed.

"A change of plans? What next?" Sonny wondered.

"Did you see Mimms grinning while Martin was talking?" Bo asked.

"I wasn't looking at Mimms," Sonny replied.

"He was grinning like he knows something, and it's something we won't like."

"Hey man, if we don't have to fill sandbags, then I like it," Sonny said.

"Maybe they're pulling the brigade out," Hal said, reviving last month's rumor that the brigade was being recalled to the states.

"Yeah, right man. I wouldn't hold your breath," Tennessee said.

"Whatever's going on, I'm not sure I like the feel of it," Hal said.

"How about some cards? We might as well do something while we wait to find out," Bo said.

"Might as well," Sonny agreed.

"And not hearts," Bo added, as they descended into the sanctuary of the bunker.

The outlook of mail and a hot meal made the day's heat and dust almost acceptable. They played cards, traded shifts guarding the bridge, and took naps as the day droned on in its excruciatingly slow and familiar cycle. When the jeep finally returned, much later than was customary, they were assembled expectantly. They received the marmite cans, the thermos of coffee, and most precious of all, the stack of mail.

116

Sonny held the mail, and the others were beginning to close around him, when Lieutenant Edmonds announced, "Men, tomorrow you'll be moving up to the Hill."

They stood dumbfounded, looking at the lieutenant.

"Move up to the Hill, sir?" Sonny finally asked. "Who'll be guarding the bridge?"

"These two bridges have been re-classified as non-essential," Lieutenant Edmonds replied. "We're short-handed on the Hill, and we're pulling both bridges."

"Tomorrow morning you will have all ammunition and gear ready," Sergeant Martin told them. "A truck will be coming from battalion to pick you up and bring you to the Hill. The Engineers will be here later to bulldoze the bunker."

"What's to keep the VC from blowing the bridge?" Sonny asked.

"That won't be your concern," Sergeant Martin replied. He smiled at them triumphantly and puffed on his cigar. "Your little vacation out here is over."

They stood in shock, watching the jeep recede. "Oh fuck," Tennessee cursed. "I don't believe this shit!"

"This is fucked up, man. Non-essential? I don't believe it," Hal said.

"We're going to get stuck with the shit now," Sonny sighed.

"Those lifers are crazy," Bo said. "First we're going to build a new bunker, and now they're going to bulldoze it instead. They're nuts!"

"This is the Army, man. What do you expect?" Sonny said.

They set aside their frustration long enough to receive the letters that Sonny handed out. "Damn, even *I* got one," he said, beaming. "What's for supper, Bo?" he asked.

"Beef stew with corn bread, and it smells damn good."

They tore into their letters, and the bunker grew quiet as each forgot his immediate concerns and poured over these words from home.

"Damn, my brother got arrested at an anti-war demonstration," Hal declared. "Get this. The little shit hand-cuffed himself to a building!"

"You'd better quit sending him pot in the mail. The dude can't handle it," Sonny said.

"Geez, what a nut," Hal said, shaking his head.

Once they had read their letters, they scooped hot stew into their mess-kits. They ate in silence, reading the letters over again while there was still enough light.

"It doesn't look like the kids are coming for a meal," observed Sonny.

"They're really going to think we're shit-heads when they find out we're up and leaving," Hal said.

"Hell, the VC will blow these bridges the first night," Tennessee said.

"Charlie won't blow the bridges," Sonny said. "Hell, they know they're winning. If they blow the bridges, they'll just have to rebuild them."

"What about the village?" Hal asked.

"Like I said, they've been going at it for more than thirty years, man. They'll get by."

"If this bridge is so non-essential, I'd like to know what the fuck we've been doing here for the last three months," Tennessee said.

"It was essential back then, Bo," Bo said, laughing.

"Yeah, man. The bridge just got Vietnamized. Dig it," Sonny said.

"I don't know if I can handle being around Martin all day. I just know he's got some special shit planned for us," Tennessee said.

"Don't worry. You'll be so busy, you won't even notice him," Bo said.

Sonny spread the last of his opium onto Bombers, and they sat up smoking late into the night, as if reluctant to end their final night at the bridge.

After breakfast the next morning, they started gathering up ammo boxes, picking up claymores from the perimeter, and packing their personal belongings, making a pile in front of the bunker.

A knot of kids from the village gathered at a distance to watch them, attracted by the unusual activity.

When all the gear had been stockpiled and there was yet no sign of the truck, Hal suggested, "We might as well get some pictures of the place before we go."

"Good idea," Tennessee agreed, and they got their cameras out.

They snapped pictures of each other standing on the bridge flashing peace signs, and standing next to the milepost, each pointing to his hometown.

Tuan and Tim walked up to them as they stood on the bridge looking down into the water. "What you do?" Tuan asked.

"Hi Tommy," said Hal. "We go to the Hill," he said, pointing down the highway.

The boys' eyes grew wide with surprise. "You go? Why you go?" asked Tuan.

"The lifers say we must go."

"Who stay here now?" Tuan asked.

"Nobody stay here now." Hal felt awkward and shabby with his inadequate response.

"You afraid of VC," Tim cried in a shrill, accusing voice.

"We have no say in it," Sonny told them. "We no want to go."

"You afraid of VC! You afraid!" Tuan shouted.

"No, no Tommy," said Hal, shaken and not sure what to say. "Tommy, here," he said, and he took the harmonica from his pocket. "Here, I souvenir you." He handed the harmonica to Tuan.

Tuan held the harmonica, turning it in his hand. He looked up at Hal and regarded him. Tuan's glare was not that of a young boy, but seemed directed, instead, from eyes forged and aged by a long history of oppression. "My name no Tommy," he finally said. He flung the harmonica over the bridge. "My name Tuan!" he cried. With tears running down his cheeks, he turned and ran.

Hal watched the harmonica arc from Tuan's hand, plummet into the creek, and drop out of sight beneath the brown water. The calls of Tuan and Tim as they ran to the village rang in his ears. "Lifah! Lifah! Lifah!" they called.

The End

Made in the USA
San Bernardino, CA
14 January 2017